# MAGIC puppy

## A new Beginning & Muddy Paws

## SUE BENTLEY

### Illustrated by Angela Swan

PUFFIN

PUFFIN BOOKS

Published by the Penguin Group
Penguin Books Ltd, 80 Strand, London WC2R ORL, England
Penguin Group (USA) Inc., 375 Hudson Street, New York, New York 10014, USA
Penguin Group (Canada), 90 Eglinton Avenue East, Suite 700, Toronto, Ontario, Canada M4P 2Y3
(a division of Pearson Penguin Canada Inc.)
Penguin Ireland, 25 St Stephen's Green, Dublin 2, Ireland (a division of Penguin Books Ltd)
Penguin Group (Australia), 250 Camberwell Road, Camberwell, Victoria 3124, Australia
(a division of Pearson Australia Group Pty Ltd)
Penguin Books India Pvt Ltd, 11 Community Centre, Panchsheel Park, New Delhi – 110 017, India
Penguin Group (NZ), 67 Apollo Drive, Rosedale, Auckland 0632, New Zealand
(a division of Pearson New Zealand Ltd)
Penguin Books (South Africa) (Pty) Ltd, 24 Sturdee Avenue, Rosebank,
Johannesburg 2196, South Africa

Penguin Books Ltd, Registered Offices: 80 Strand, London WC2R ORL, England

puffinbooks.com

Magic Puppy: A New Beginning first published 2008
Magic Puppy: Muddy Paws first published 2008
First published in one volume 2011

003

Text copyright © Sue Bentley, 2008
Illustrations copyright © Angela Swan, 2008
All rights reserved

The moral right of the author and illustrator has been asserted

Set in Bembo by Palimpsest Book Production Limited, Falkirk, Stirlingshire
Made and printed in Great Britain by Clays Ltd, St Ives plc

British Library Cataloguing in Publication Data
A CIP catalogue record for this book is available from the British Library

ISBN: 978-0-141-33916-0

www.greenpenguin.co.uk

MIX
Paper from
responsible sources
FSC   FSC™ C018179
www.fsc.org

Penguin Books is committed to a sustainable
future for our business, our readers and our planet.
This book is made from Forest Stewardship
Council™ certified paper.

ALWAYS LEARNING          **PEARSON**

# My dearest puppy, Storm,

I hope this letter reaches you safe and sound. You have been so brave since you had to flee from the evil wolf Shadow.

Do not worry about me. I will hide here until you are strong enough to return and lead our pack. For now you must move on – you must hide from Shadow and his spies. If Shadow finds this letter I believe he will try to destroy it . . .

Find a good friend – someone to help finish my message to you. Because what I have to say to you is important. What I have to say is this: you must always

Please don't feel lonely. Trust in your friends and all will be well.

Your loving mother,

Canista

Sue Bentley's books for children often include animals, fairies and wildlife. She lives in Northampton and enjoys reading, going to the cinema, relaxing by her garden pond and watching the birds feeding their babies on the lawn. At school she was always getting told off for daydreaming or staring out of the window – but she now realizes that she was storing up ideas for when she became a writer. She has met and owned many cats and dogs, and each one has brought a special kind of magic to her life.

# MAGIC puppy

## A New Beginning

*To Cindy – first and best-beloved,*
*who was happy in a doll's pram*

# Prologue

Storm whimpered as he crawled into
the cave. Behind the young silver-grey
wolf, stars glimmered in the purple sky.

Suddenly, a piercing howl echoed on
the night air.

'Shadow!' Storm gasped, trembling
with fear.

The fierce lone wolf who had
attacked the Moon-claw pack was close

by. Storm must disguise himself, and quickly!

There was a dazzling gold flash and a fountain of golden sparks that lit up the back of the cave for a brief second. Where the wolf cub had stood, there now crouched a tiny, sandy golden retriever puppy with floppy ears and twinkling midnight-blue eyes.

Storm's little puppy heart beat fast. In that split second of light, he had seen the she-wolf lying crumpled against a rock.

'Mother?' he whined, plunging deeper into the cave.

'Storm?' Canista lifted her head to answer him in a velvety growl.

In the dim light Storm could see his

mother's heaving sides and hear her rapid breathing. He felt a new surge of panic. 'You are hurt! Did Shadow attack you too?'

Canista nodded weakly. 'His bite is poisoned. It drains my strength.'

Storm's blue eyes flared with sorrow and anger. 'He has already killed my father and my three litter brothers. I will face Shadow and fight him!'

'Bravely said, my son. But now is not the time. You are the only cub left of our Moon-claw pack. Go to the other world. Use this disguise to hide. Return when your magic is stronger. Then, together, we will fight Shadow.' Canista's head flopped back tiredly as she finished speaking.

Storm bowed his head. He did not

want to leave her, but he knew his mother was right.

The sound of mighty paws and a thunderous snarl echoed from the mouth of the cave.

'Go, Storm. Save yourself,' Canista growled urgently.

Storm's sandy fur ignited with gold sparks. He whined softly as he felt the power building inside him. The golden light around him grew brighter. And brighter . . .

# ★ Chapter ★
# ONE

Lily Benson felt a leap of excitement as her dad drew up outside Greengates riding stables.

'Yay! I love Saturday afternoons. I get to spend hours and hours with ponies!' she cried, jumping out of the car.

Lily went round to the open window and bent down to kiss her dad's cheek.

Mr Benson laughed. 'Careful you don't get pony-overload!'

'There's no such thing,' Lily said firmly. Her bedroom walls were covered with posters of ponies and her bookcase was crammed with riding books and magazines.

'Shame. I was hoping you might stop pestering your mum and me to buy you one!' her dad said.

He was only joking, but Lily felt a pang. She was desperate for a pony of her own. But her parents were worried about the hard work and amount of time it would take to look after it. Lily knew they were hoping she'd be satisfied with having free rides in exchange for helping out at Greengates.

'I'll never stop asking in a zillion years. Ponies rule, Dad!' she said.

'You've got a one-track mind, Lily Benson. Have a good time. See you later,' he called, steering away from the kerb.

Lily sighed. She waved goodbye and then went into the stable yard.

The main stable buildings were built around two sides of a square. A large gate at one end led to the paddock. Just beyond the paddock Lily could see the cottage where Janie Green who ran Greengates lived.

Janie was outside the tack room with Treacle and Taffy, two of the smaller ponies. Two young children in riding gear stood waiting ready to mount.

Janie looked up and smiled warmly as

Lily approached. She had a round pretty face with twinkling brown eyes and was always cheerful. 'Hi, Lily. I hope you're feeling energetic. We're fully booked this afternoon.'

'Hi, Janie,' Lily said. She patted Taffy's neck and stroked Treacle's nose. 'What do you want me to do first?'

'You could give Don a hand with the mucking out, if you don't mind. He's over at Bandit's stall,' Janie said.

'OK,' Lily said happily. Bandit was her favourite pony. She was a sweet-natured palomino with a golden-tan coat and a pale mane and tail. Lily would have loved to own a pony just like her.

As Lily went off to find the stable lad she saw even more young riders arriving with their parents. It looked

like it was going to be a hectic
afternoon.

Lily said hello to Bandit for a few
minutes, before spending the next hour
or so forking up droppings, wheeling
them over to the muck heap and
spreading fresh bedding.

Riders and ponies came and went.

Lily lent a hand where it was needed. It was a hot day and she was soon red-faced and sweaty.

'Why don't you take a break and go and get a drink?' Don suggested, as she helped him fill the hay nets and water buckets. He was tall and wiry, with dark-red hair, freckles and a thin face.

'Phew! I think I will,' Lily said, pushing a strand of damp blonde hair back from her forehead.

She went to the stable's kitchen and had a long, cold drink of orange juice.

As Lily was sauntering back past the paddock, she noticed some litter blowing about on the grass and went to pick it up.

'Thanks for that, Lily. You're doing a grand job!' Janie Green called, pausing to rest the heavy saddle she was carrying on the paddock fence.

'It makes me so mad when people leave stuff about. Don't they care that a plastic bag could kill a pony if it eats it?' Lily said indignantly.

'I don't suppose they give it a thought. Maybe they'd be more careful if they did – but not everyone's into horses.'

Lily shrugged. 'That's their loss, then!'

'I'm with you on that!' Janie said, smiling. 'Have you persuaded your parents to buy you a pony yet?'

Lily pulled a face, thinking miserably of the earlier conversation with her dad.

'I take it that's a sore point,' Janie said.

Lily nodded. 'I still have to convince

them that I can fit looking after a pony
round my schoolwork. Mum and Dad
think it would be too much for me and
I should wait until I'm older.'

'They could be right, you know,' Janie
said gently. 'Looking after a pony is a
big commitment and there are no days
off.'

Lily felt her spirits sink. She'd thought
Janie would be on her side!

'How do you fancy taking Bandit
out? We've just had a cancellation, so
she's free for a couple of hours,' Janie
said.

Lily brightened immediately at the
thought of a longer free ride than usual.
'Really? I can take her out by myself?'
she asked delightedly.

Janie nodded. 'You've ridden her

plenty of times and she's used to you. You can take her along the bridle paths, but don't go beyond the woods. OK?'

Lily nodded, feeling proud that Janie trusted her. 'Thanks, Janie! That's brilliant!'

She dashed straight across to Bandit, who was already tacked up. 'Hello, girl. We're going for a ride,' she crooned, stroking the pony's nose.

Bandit gave a friendly whicker and nuzzled Lily's palm. Lily buckled on her riding hat before mounting the palomino pony and using her heels to nudge her forward.

They trotted out of Greengates and turned on to the bridle path that ran down the edge of a field. The path

branched further on and Lily took the
way to the woods.

Other riders from the stables passed
her on their way back.

As she and Bandit entered the shade
of the trees, Lily's mind drifted into a
wonderful daydream. It was easy to
imagine that Bandit was her own pony
and they were quite alone. The sound
of other riders was muffled and she was

screened from them by the thick bushes. Sunlight filtered through the leaves and speckled everything with spots of light.

'I wish you were mine,' Lily said dreamily, leaning forward to pat Bandit's satiny neck.

Suddenly Bandit stumbled on a tree root and the reins were jerked right out of Lily's hands.

'Oh!' Lily pitched forward and shot straight over the pony's neck. As the ground rushed up to meet her she closed her eyes, ready for the painful landing.

# ★ Chapter ★
# TWO

The collision with the ground never came.

With a dazzling golden flash and a crackle of sparks, Lily found herself jerking to a sudden halt. Her eyes flew open in shock and she saw that she was caught inside a huge glowing golden net, in mid-air, half a metre above the ground!

Very slowly, Lily felt herself float down and land gently on some bracken. With a fizzing noise, the glowing net broke up into golden sparks and then melted away into the leaves.

Lily sat up, blinking confusedly. Her first thought was for Bandit. She whipped round and was relieved to see the pony nibbling some grass in a small clearing a few metres away.

'Your riding creature is fine. I hope that you are not injured,' said a strange voice.

Lily stiffened. 'W-who said that?'

A tiny puppy with sandy fur, floppy ears and huge midnight-blue eyes crawled out from beneath a frond of bracken. 'I did. My name is Storm of the Moon-claw pack. What are you?

And what is the name of your pack?' it woofed.

Lily's jaw dropped as she stared at the puppy in utter amazement. She felt like pinching herself to make sure she wasn't dreaming. But she saw that the puppy was looking at her quizzically as if waiting for her to respond.

'I'm a g-girl. A human . . . I'm L-Lily. Lily Benson,' she found herself

stammering. 'But I don't know what you mean about a pack.'

'A human? I have heard of these.' Storm's silky forehead wrinkled in a frown. Lily saw that he was beginning to tremble. 'Can I trust you, Lily? I come from far away and I need your help.'

Lily was still having difficulty taking this in, but she didn't want to frighten this amazing puppy away. He was absolutely gorgeous with the brightest midnight-blue eyes she had ever seen and big soft paws that looked too big for his body.

Very slowly she got up on to her knees and reached out her hand.

To Lily's delight, Storm edged closer and brushed her fingers with his damp little nose. His tail wagged nervously.

Despite being so scared, the tiny puppy seemed to trust her.

'Why do you need my help?' she asked gently.

Storm's deep-blue eyes flashed with anger and sadness. 'A lone wolf called Shadow attacked us. My father and brothers were killed and my mother is sick and in hiding. Shadow wants to lead the Moon-claw wolf pack, but the others will not follow him as long as I am alive.'

'*Wolf* pack? But you're a pup–' Lily stopped as Storm held up a velvety sandy paw and began backing away.

There was another dazzling bright flash and a burst of gold sparks showered over Lily, crackling around her feet on the ground.

'Oh!' Lily rubbed her eyes, blinded
for a second. When she could see again,
she saw that the tiny sandy puppy had
gone. In its place now stood a majestic
young wolf with thick silver-grey fur
and glowing midnight-blue eyes.

'Storm?' Lily gasped, eyeing the wolf's
large teeth and thick neck-ruff that
glimmered with hundreds of gold sparks
like tiny yellow diamonds.

'Yes, Lily, it is me,' Storm said in a
deep velvety growl.

Before Lily could get used to seeing Storm as his magnificent real self, there was a final gold flash and he appeared once again as a cute sandy puppy.

'Wow! You really are a wolf. That's a brilliant disguise,' she said, getting up from her knees.

Storm began trembling again. 'Not if Shadow's magic finds me. Will you help me to hide?'

Lily's heart went out to the helpless puppy. 'Of course I will. You can live with . . .' She tailed off as she remembered her parents' rules about having no house pets as they were out all day. They'd probably insist on taking Storm to the pet care centre. There must be some way she could help the tiny puppy. 'Maybe I could smuggle you

into my house, but I don't see how I
can hide you for long,' she said
thoughtfully.

'Do not worry. I will use my magic
so that only you will be able to see and
hear me,' Storm woofed.

'You can make yourself invisible?
Wow!' Lily breathed. 'No problem, then.
You're coming straight home with me.
Just let me catch Bandit. By the time

we get back to Greengates, it'll be time for Dad to pick me up.'

A few minutes later, as she cradled Storm in her lap on Bandit's back, a big smile spread across Lily's face. Never in her wildest dreams had she imagined having a magic puppy for a friend!

# ★ Chapter ★
# THREE

'You should sleep in here in case Mum or Dad gets suspicious,' Lily told Storm, spreading an old jumper in the bottom of her wardrobe. 'But when no one's around, you can get on my bed.'

Storm looked in the wardrobe and then padded around her bedroom, sniffing everything and exploring. 'This is a good place.'

'Glad you like it!' Lily said, beaming at him. 'Are you hungry?'

The tiny puppy barked eagerly.

'OK. I'll go and raid the kitchen to see what I can find. I won't be long.'

Lily dashed downstairs. Luckily her dad was in the garden cutting the lawn and her mum had just gone out to her yoga class. She found some leftover chicken in the fridge and quickly broke a piece off for Storm.

Back upstairs, she watched as Storm ate hungrily and then sat back licking his lips. 'That was delicious. I like human food.'

'I'll get you some proper food later,' Lily said.

Storm nodded. 'Good. We will go hunting together!'

'I couldn't do that!' Lily said,
horrified. 'Anyway, there's no need. The
shop at the end of the street sells dog
food in tins. I'll buy some with my
pocket money,' she told him.

Storm yawned, showing his sharp
little teeth. 'I think that I will rest now.'
Padding over to the wardrobe, he curled
up on the old jumper with a contented
sigh and promptly went to sleep.

Lily watched the tiny puppy's furry

sides rising and falling. Almost at once his paws twitched as he started dreaming. *He must be exhausted from his long journey*, she thought, already feeling fond of him.

Leaving Storm to sleep, Lily reached for a book of pony stories and stretched out on her tummy on her bed to read.

The book was really good and she hardly noticed time passing. She was halfway through an exciting story about a pony being stolen, when something leapt on to her bed and launched itself on top of her.

Lily almost jumped out of her skin. 'Storm! You scared me!' she said, laughing as she rolled over on to her back. 'Did you have a good snooze?'

'Yes, thank you. I feel safe here with you,' Storm woofed happily. Plonking his big soft paws on her book, he leaned up and began licking her chin.

Lily wrapped her arms round his plump little sandy body and gave him a cuddle. After a couple of minutes, Storm squirmed free and sprang on to the rug with a surprisingly loud thud for a tiny puppy.

'I would like to go outside now!'

'OK,' Lily said, getting up off the bed. 'Our garden's not very big, but there's a field nearby. I'll take you for a walk over there.'

Storm gave an eager little bark and followed her downstairs.

As they reached the hall, her dad appeared at the sitting-room door. He had a frown on his face. 'What was all that thumping about upstairs? It sounded like a herd of elephants.'

'Dad! I . . . er . . . thought you were outside,' Lily gasped in panic.

She quickly shifted about, trying to stand in front of Storm before she suddenly remembered that he was invisible. Then, realizing how strange that must look, she began bending and stretching her arms. 'Whew! Whew!'

she puffed for added emphasis. 'Just
doing a few exercises. I'm trying to get
fit. I was about to come and tell you
that I'm going out for a jog around the
field!'

Her dad raised his eyebrows as Lily
did a star jump. 'Well, I guess that's a
good idea. Maybe I'll come with you.
I could do with some exercise too.'

'No!' Lily said hastily. 'Someone . . .
um . . . from school might see me. I'll

look a real baby if I'm trailing around after you.'

'Pardon me for trying to cramp your style,' her dad joked. 'What's brought this new fitness fad on?'

'I want to be ready for when I get my own pony, don't I? It's going to be hard work looking after it,' Lily replied cheekily.

Her dad rolled his eyes. 'I might have known what was at the bottom of this! Do you ever think of anything else beside ponies?'

'Nope! Well, actually, yes! But you wouldn't believe me if I told you!' Lily said, glancing at Storm who was waiting by the front door. She jogged towards him before her dad could ask any more awkward questions. 'See you later!'

# ★ Chapter ★
# FOUR

As Lily put her school books into her
bag on Monday morning, Storm sat
watching her.

She smiled at him. 'I love having you
living here with me, but I have to go
out for a few hours. Try not to get
bored and chew my rug or anything,
or Mum will freak!'

'I will not do anything like that,'
Storm yapped indignantly.

'Sorry. Sometimes I forget you're not
an ordinary puppy,' Lily said, bending
down to stroke his silky ears. 'It's a
shame there was only time for a
quick walk around the field before
breakfast. I'll take you out for a
mega-long walk when I get back
from school. Promise.'

Storm looked up at her curiously.
'What is school?'

'It's a place where kids go to learn.
Teachers tell us stuff and give us
homework to do and we do projects
and all kinds of things,' Lily explained.

'School sounds interesting. I will
come with you,' Storm decided.

Lily grinned. 'I wish you could, but pets
aren't allowed . . .' She paused as she had
a second thought. 'Hey! Maybe you *can*
come if you stay invisible! But you'd have
to keep really quiet and stay close to me.
Mr Poke, our class teacher, is very strict.'

Storm's face brightened and his
little sandy tail started wagging with
excitement. 'I will make sure that no one
will know I'm there – except you, Lily!'

'Cool! Let's go!' Lily put her school

bag on the floor and opened it up. 'It might be best if you got inside. I have to cross some busy roads.'

Storm jumped into her bag and settled next to her books and gym kit. Lily shouldered her bag, said goodbye to her parents and headed out of the front door.

'We'll probably meet Freema and Katy, my friends from class, on the way. I can't wait to see their faces when I tell them about you!' she said to Storm.

There was a scuffling noise from her bag. Storm popped his head out, his big dewy eyes looking into Lily's. 'You cannot tell anyone my secret. Promise me, Lily,' he woofed seriously.

Lily was disappointed. She had always

wanted a pet to tell her friends about, especially a pony, but she had been really excited at the thought that she might be able to share her amazing magic puppy friend. She'd do anything if it would help keep Storm safe, though. 'OK, I promise. Cross my heart and hope to die,' she said.

Storm nodded, satisfied.

As Lily and Storm reached the school gate, they saw Freema and Katy. There was another girl with them whom Lily hadn't seen before.

'Hi, Katy. Hi, Freema,' Lily greeted her friends.

'Hi, Lily. This is my cousin, Adjoa,' Freema explained. 'She's just moved here and is going to be in our class.'

Adjoa was tall with springy black hair,

an oval face and big brown eyes, just
like Freema.

Lily smiled at her. 'Welcome to our
school, Adjoa.'

'Thanks,' Adjoa said shyly.

'Did you help out at Greengates this
weekend?' Katy asked Lily as they
walked into the school grounds.

Lily nodded. 'It was great. I had an
extra-long ride on Bandit. Janie let
me take her up to the woods by myself.'

'Cool!' Katy said.

'Do you like riding?' Adjoa asked Lily.

'It's my favourite thing ever in the
whole world!' Lily replied. 'How about
you?'

'Adjoa's pony-mad,' Freema said. She
nudged her cousin. 'Tell Lily about your
pony.'

Lily's eyes widened. 'You've got your own pony? You lucky thing! What's its name?'

'Pixie. She's gorgeous and I love her to bits,' Adjoa said. 'You can come round one night after school and meet her if you like.'

'Thanks. I'd love to,' Lily said, beaming.

In the classroom, Lily took her usual seat next to Katy. She put her bag on the floor, so that Storm could jump out.

Storm gave himself a shake and then trotted off to sniff around the room.

Mr Poke took the register. 'And just before we begin,' he said, looking up, 'I'd like to welcome Adjoa Hardiker to the class.'

Adjoa smiled shyly as everyone clapped, including Lily.

A few minutes later, Lily was leaning over to watch Storm. She smiled to herself as the tiny puppy weaved in and out of the desks, his sandy tail wagging.

A voice called out, but Lily was engrossed by Storm's cute antics.

'Lily Benson, can you stop daydreaming and take out your history book, please?' the teacher's sarcastic voice said. Mr Poke had a bald head with a fuzzy rim of hair round his ears. He had a way of looking down his nose when he was annoyed.

Lily's head snapped up. 'Sorry, sir.'

'Looks like old Poker Face got out of bed the wrong side – again,' Katy commented. Adjoa and Freema, who sat nearby, giggled.

Lily turned round and grinned at them.

'Right, class. I'd like you to begin work on your projects, please. Quietly, if possible!' Mr Poke ordered.

They were doing the Tudors. Lily was making a collage of Queen Elizabeth I. 'I think I'll do her lace ruff today. I need to get some bits of paper and stuff from the art cupboard,' she said to Katy, who was bent over writing in her notebook.

'Can we have a bit more work and a little less talking, Lily Benson?' Mr Poke drawled.

'Yes, sir.' Lily felt herself going pink as she got up and went to the cupboard. *I wasn't even doing anything*, she thought.

Storm padded over to her. 'Are you all right, Lily? You look hot,' he woofed.

'I'm fine. Not like *some* people,' Lily murmured, glancing back at the grumpy teacher.

She pulled the cupboard's handle, but it seemed to have stuck. Grasping it more firmly, she pulled again, but the door still wouldn't budge.

'I will help,' Storm yapped eagerly.

Lily saw Mr Poke coming over with a frown on his face. 'Uh-oh, you'd better be quick, Storm. Looks like Poker Face is on the war path,' she whispered.

Lily felt an odd, warm tingling down her spine as gold sparks ignited in Storm's sandy coat, and the tips of his ears and tail fizzed with power. Something strange was going to happen.

Raising one big sandy front paw,
Storm sent a shower of bright golden
sparks whooshing towards the cupboard.
With a faint crackle they sank into the
wood. For a moment nothing happened
and Lily thought Storm's magic hadn't
worked.

'Out of the way, Lily. Let me do it,' Mr
Poke said irritably, reaching the cupboard
– just as the doors sprang open.

An explosion of papers, brushes, pens
and paints shot out. Mr Poke flew
backwards as if he'd been blown by a
wind machine and landed on the floor
on his backside.

*Rustle!* Papers floated down around
him. *Splat!* A plastic pot of glue hit Mr
Poke on the chest, bursting and
spreading all over his grey jumper.

*Thwack!* Brushes, pens and pencils pinged at him, sticking firmly to the glue.

The teacher sat there blinking in shock.

The whole class erupted with laughter. Katy, Adjoa and Freema were helpless.

Lily tried hard to bite back the laugh bubbling up inside her.

'Whoever packed the cupboard like

that?' Mr Poke roared, his face bright
red as he scrambled to his feet. 'I'll
have to go and get cleaned up. Get
on with your work, class. I'll be
right back.' He stomped off towards
the cloakroom, shedding pens and
pencils with a clatter as he went.

'I am sorry, Lily. I think I used too
much magic,' Storm woofed in
dismay.

Making sure that no one was looking,
Lily quickly patted him. 'You did just
fine. It serves Mr Poke right!'

She began putting everything back
into the cupboard. Katy, Freema and
Adjoa helped her. By the time Mr Poke
reappeared wearing a hideous orange,
yellow and brown striped T-shirt, the
mess was all cleared up.

The rest of the morning passed quickly, and at lunchtime Lily shared her cheese sandwiches and crisps with Storm. When they'd eaten, she took him for a run across the playing fields. The excited puppy tore about, chasing leaves in the wind and tiring himself out. He spent the rest of the afternoon dozing under Lily's chair.

After school, with Storm once again in her bag, Lily walked home with her friends.

She paused at the end of her road. 'Did you mean it about me coming round to see Pixie?' she asked Adjoa.

Adjoa nodded. 'Why don't you come round after school on Friday? We can both ride Pixie if you like.'

'That would be brilliant!' Lily said.

She jotted Adjoa's address and phone
number in her notebook before heading
for home. 'Bye. See you all tomorrow!'
she called.

Katy, Freema and Adjoa waved as they
walked away.

Just inside her front garden, Lily put
her bag down so that Storm could
jump out. 'Adjoa's nice, isn't she?' she
said to him. 'I can't wait to meet Pixie.'

'Me too!' Storm nodded, his pink
tongue lolling in a doggy grin.

47

Lily felt a surge of affection for him. She picked Storm up and stroked his soft sandy fur. 'Having you at school today was brilliant! You really taught old Poker Face a lesson. I hope that horrible Shadow never finds you and then you can live with me forever and come to school every day,' she said.

'That is not possible, Lily,' Storm told her, his small sandy face suddenly serious. 'One day I must return to my own world to help heal my mother and fight Shadow.'

Lily knew this was true, but she didn't want to believe it. She pushed all thoughts of Storm having to leave from her mind and thought instead of the fun they would have on Friday with Adjoa and Pixie.

# ★ Chapter ★
# FIVE

'Here you are, girl.' Lily held a piece of carrot on the flat of her hand, so that Pixie could take it with her soft lips. Pixie was a chestnut pony with a white blaze down her nose and a friendly expression.

Lily turned to Adjoa as the pony crunched the treat. 'Pixie's absolutely gorgeous!'

Adjoa smiled. 'I know. I'm lucky to have her.'

Pixie whinnied softly and swivelled her ears.

'I think she agrees with you,' Lily said. They both laughed.

Adjoa opened the field gate and Lily helped her saddle the pony and then both girls spent a happy couple of hours taking it in turns to ride her. Lily thought with a sigh how wonderful it would be to have her own pony and ride her every day.

Storm bounded alongside the pony at first as Lily trotted around the field on her, but his short legs soon got tired. Lily couldn't lift him into her lap with Adjoa watching. 'Are you OK? You're not getting bored?' she leaned down to whisper to him.

'I am fine. I will go and explore,' Storm barked softly.

Lily watched him go gambolling off towards the open-sided, wooden shelter at the bottom of the field. She could see him sniffing all the interesting smells in patches of long grass on the way.

With Storm happily occupied, Lily went back to enjoying her ride. Afterwards she helped Adjoa untack Pixie and then rub her down before letting her run free. The pony immediately threw herself on to her back and had a good roll. Storm ran straight up to her barking happily.

'Oh no!' Lily gasped, only just
stopping herself from calling out to
warn Storm to be careful. If Pixie
kicked out, the tiny puppy could get
badly hurt by her hooves.

'What's wrong?' Adjoa asked, frowning.

'Er . . . nothing,' Lily murmured,
watching tensely as Pixie got to her
feet again and shook herself. Her ears
flattened as she looked down at the
playful puppy, then she leaned down
and gently snuffled Storm's sandy fur.
Storm yapped delightedly, wagging his
tail.

Lily gave a big sigh of relief, which she quickly turned into a cough. She turned to Adjoa. 'Sorry. I . . . um . . . thought I saw a rat scrabbling in the straw in Pixie's shelter!'

Adjoa shrugged. 'That's no big deal. The farmer's cats will catch it. Let's go in the house and get a drink.' She opened the field gate that led straight into her back garden.

'OK. I'll follow you in a sec. I think I've got a stone in my boot.' Bending down so that she had her back to Adjoa, Lily beckoned to Storm.

Storm scampered straight over and squeezed under the fence into the back garden. He trotted at Lily's heel, panting happily as they all walked towards the house.

In the kitchen, Adjoa's mum was getting cold drinks from the fridge. 'I saw you coming,' she said, smiling. 'You must be Lily. It's nice to meet you. I'm glad Adjoa's already made a new friend.' Her rows of tiny black plaits were pinned up into a bun. She wore gold hoop earrings, jeans and a pretty green top.

'Thanks for the drink, Mrs Hardiker,' Lily said politely.

After their drinks, Lily and Storm went up to Adjoa's room. 'It's just like mine!' Lily said delightedly, looking at all the pony posters and books. Red and blue rosettes that Adjoa had won for her riding were pinned round her mirror.

'That was brilliant fun! Thanks,'

Lily said to Adjoa, before she left for home.

'That's OK. You can come here any time,' Adjoa said, smiling. 'See you at school on Monday!'

As she walked away with Storm, Lily was thoughtful. 'Adjoa's mum and dad don't seem to have a problem with their daughter looking after a pony and doing schoolwork. But I don't think I'll *ever* persuade mine to let me have one,' she said to him with a sigh.

Storm whined in sympathy, wagging his tail. His thick sandy fur gleamed with tiny golden sparks. 'Maybe I can help you,' he woofed softly.

★

The following afternoon, Mrs Benson dropped Lily and Storm off early at Greengates before she went to her yoga workshop. Lily had been silently mulling over what Storm had said; now she was bursting to ask him about it.

'Did you mean it, about helping me to get my own pony?' she asked as they walked across the stable yard.

Storm looked at her with alert midnight-blue eyes. 'I did, Lily. I always keep my promises.'

Lily waited, but Storm didn't say anything more. Her imagination went into overdrive. 'I bet you're going to use your magic to make a pony appear out of thin air, aren't you? Are you

going to put Mum and Dad into a
trance or something, so they let me
keep it?' she asked excitedly.

Storm's furry brow dipped in a
frown. 'No. That would not be the
right thing to do, Lily. I am afraid that
you will have to be patient,' he woofed
mysteriously. He leapt forward and

went off to explore the yard, shedding
a few tiny gold sparks, which glinted
in the bright sunlight before dissolving.

Lily stared after Storm. She knew she
was going to have to do as he said, but
it was hard to be patient when you
wanted something so much.

It was time that she went to see what
jobs needed doing, but first Lily went
to visit Bandit. She had an apple in her
pocket for the pony.

But the palomino wasn't in her loose
box, so Lily went to check the paddock.
Bandit wasn't there either. As she was
walking back across the yard feeling
puzzled, Don came out of the tack
room holding a saddle.

'Is Bandit out on an early ride?' Lily
asked the stable lad.

'No. Bandit's already gone. Didn't Janie tell you?' Don said.

'Gone? Gone where?' Lily asked.

'To her new home,' Don explained. 'Bandit's quite old now and Janie's been thinking about retiring her for some time. Someone came by in the week and offered Bandit a new home on the spot. Janie jumped at it. Bandit's gone to live in a field with two goats and a donkey for company.'

'Oh, she'll really love that,' Lily said, trying hard not to feel sad. But she knew she was really going to miss the gentle old pony.

Don's freckled face crinkled in a smile. 'It's amazing that somewhere so perfect came right out of the blue, when Janie hadn't really started looking yet. Just like magic, really. Anyway, see you later.' He went off to tack up a pony.

Storm came rushing across the yard, with a dusty nose from where he'd been rooting about in some straw. He gave her a wide doggy grin and flopped down at her feet.

Lily looked down at him thoughtfully. 'Did you have anything to do with finding Bandit a perfect new home, by any chance?'

Storm gave her a cheeky sideways look. He twitched his nose. 'I smell rabbits!' he yapped happily and shot off again towards the paddock.

Lily stared after him. He was up to something, she was sure of it.

# ★ Chapter ★
# SIX

It had been another busy afternoon at Greengates. Lily was hanging up a pile of newly cleaned bridles in the tack room.

Janie popped her head round the door. 'Why don't you leave that now and go and have a ride? Tinka's still saddled up.'

'Thanks, Janie!' Glancing over to

where Storm was snoozing on top of the brush box, Lily called to him. 'Come on, Storm. Walkies!'

'That is my favourite word!' Storm's head shot up immediately. He jumped down and padded after Lily to where Tinka was tied to the hitching rail.

Lily buckled on her riding hat before mounting the handsome bay pony. She walked Tinka out of the yard and on to the bridle path. This time she took the fork leading to a field that the riding school had permission to use. Storm

loped along beside her, his ears flapping
as Lily rode down a tractor track.

Lily had to concentrate quite hard
when riding Tinka. The bay pony was
less experienced than dear old Bandit
had been. Lily dismounted and was
opening the field gate, when a wood
pigeon fluttered up out of a bush.
Startled, Tinka threw up her head and
danced sideways.

'It's OK, girl.' Lily spoke reassuringly,
stroking Tinka's nose to calm her.

As Tinka backed up, Lily noticed a
ditch almost concealed in the long grass
by the hedge. Someone had dumped
some sharp hawthorn branches in it.
Luckily, Tinka had just missed it or she
could have been injured. Lily made a
mental note to tell Janie about the

dangerous ditch when she got back to Greengates.

Storm sat in her lap as Lily continued her ride. But as she made her way back an hour or so later he loped along beside her once more. She saw him run off into the field and start springing about, barking at butterflies and nosing into molehills. By the time Lily got back to the field gate and dismounted again, Storm was behind her.

Lily led Tinka through and was closing the gate, when she spotted a familiar pony and rider coming towards her along the edge of the field. 'Look, Storm! It's Adjoa on Pixie!' she cried delightedly.

A moist brown nose and then two sandy ears appeared as Storm squeezed

through a small gap in the hedge. He
gave an excited bark and leapt towards
the long grass.

Lily realized that he was heading
straight for the concealed ditch. 'Storm!
Look out!' she cried. But the puppy
was so intent on reaching his friend
Pixie that he didn't seem to have heard
her.

Lily threw herself forward. She missed
Storm, but just managed to push him

sideways as she lost her balance and slid into the ditch.

'Ow!' she gasped with pain, as her ankle twisted and sharp thorns dug into her leg.

Storm looked down at her in dismay. 'You saved me, Lily. But you are hurt. I will help you,' he whined.

'I . . . I think I'm OK,' Lily said shakily, biting back tears at the sharp ache in her leg. Her jodhpurs were torn and smeared with grass stains.

Time seemed to stand still. Lily felt a familiar warm tingling down her back as vivid gold sparks ignited in Storm's fur. His tail stiffened and crackled with power. Raising a velvety front paw Storm sent a whoosh of sparks fizzing towards Lily's injured leg. For a second

the pain increased and then it drained
away just as if someone had poured it
down a plughole.

When the bright sparks faded,
Lily saw that her jodhpurs were clean
and mended too. 'Thanks, Storm,' she
whispered.

'You are welcome,' Storm woofed as
the final gold sparks faded from his
thick sandy fur.

Lily quickly climbed out of the ditch.
She stood up as Adjoa pulled Pixie to a

halt a couple of metres away. 'Watch
out for this ditch. You can hardly see it.
I . . . er . . . nearly just slipped right
into . . .' she blustered. Lily racked her
brain for an explanation that didn't
involve Storm, but Adjoa wasn't
listening.

Her new friend's eyes were red and
puffy. It was obvious that Adjoa had
been crying. Lily felt a stir of sympathy.
What could be wrong?

Lily held Tinka by her reins and
listened with growing dismay to what
Adjoa had to say.

'The farmer who we rent Pixie's field
from is selling up and we can't find
another field nearby. Mum and Dad say
it would cost too much to put her into
livery stables where she'd be looked

after, and so we might have to sell her,'
Adjoa said tearfully.

'Oh no! Poor you,' Lily exclaimed,
putting one arm round her friend.

She knew it was expensive to have a
pony looked after by a livery stable. But
it was awful to think of Adjoa losing
her beloved pony.

Beside her Pixie gave a friendly blow
and dipped her head to nuzzle Storm
gently. The tiny puppy was lying on his
back in the grass with all four legs in
the air, showing his fat pale tummy. For
once, Lily felt too upset for Adjoa to
smile at his playful antics.

An idea came to her. She was going
to talk to her parents.

# ★ Chapter ★
# SEVEN

'I'm sorry, Lily. But my answer has to be the same,' Mrs Benson said.

They were all sitting in the kitchen on Saturday evening. Storm was lying down next to Lily's chair, invisible to everyone except her, as usual. Lily had just finished explaining about Pixie in the hope that her parents might be willing to buy the pony.

'I agree with your mum,' Mr Benson said. 'Looking after a pony is a big responsibility. We're just not sure this is the right time for you to take that on.'

'But it is, Dad! I'd be the most brilliant pony owner ever!' Lily said in her best pleading voice. 'And if we bought Pixie, Adjoa could still see her whenever she wanted.'

Her dad smiled and reached out to ruffle her hair. 'I'm sorry, honey. I feel bad for Adjoa too, but the subject's closed.'

'That's what I thought you'd say,' Lily said, sighing heavily.

All that evening and throughout Sunday, Adjoa and Pixie were on Lily's mind. On Monday, when she and Storm walked to school, they met up with Katy and Freema, but Adjoa wasn't with them.

'Where's Adjoa?' Lily asked.

'She's not coming in today. My aunt says she's got an upset tummy,' Freema explained.

'I know *why* Adjoa's tummy is upset. It's because she's so worried about what's going to happen to Pixie,' Lily said sadly.

Freema and Katy nodded.

When they reached the cloakroom, Lily hung back and let her friends go into school ahead of her. 'I wish I could think of a way to help Adjoa keep Pixie,' she whispered to Storm. 'But I've already tried Mum and Dad. I don't know what else I can do.'

Storm whined softly in sympathy and then his big midnight-blue eyes lit up.

'You could talk to the lady who runs the riding stables,' he suggested.

'Janie? I can't see what good that would do,' Lily said, frowning.

Storm barked encouragingly, wagging his tail and dancing round her feet in circles. Lily smiled. 'Well, OK then, if you're that sure it'll help. We'll pop over there tonight after school. Uh-oh! Watch out! Mr Poke's just come in. We'd better go into class!' she hissed out of the side of her mouth.

Back home after school, Lily quickly changed into her jeans and T-shirt, before dashing downstairs. She found her mum in the kitchen. 'Could you give me a lift over to Greengates, please?' she asked.

Her mum looked surprised. 'Don't you get enough of that place at weekends? Why do you want to go over there now?'

Lily thought quickly. 'Tinka was sick on Saturday. I wanted to check and see if she's any better,' she fibbed.

Mrs Benson smiled. 'That's a nice thought. You're a sweet person, Lily Benson.'

Lily blushed, feeling a bit guilty. But there was no way she could tell her mum that it was Storm's suggestion to go and talk to Janie. Anyway, it was true that she was always happy to see Tinka and all the other ponies. 'So can I get a lift?' she prompted.

Her mum nodded. 'We'll go now. I have to go to the supermarket, so I can

drop you off at Greengates and then
pick you up on my way back.'

Lily sat in the back of the car, with
Storm on her lap as they drove there.
She got out of the car at Greengates's
main entrance. 'Thanks for the lift,
Mum. I'll see you later.'

As soon as her mum had driven
away, Lily went into the yard. Storm
trotted purposefully at heel, invisible as
usual.

She could see Janie sitting at her
computer through the office window.

Lily paused, feeling a stir of
uncertainty. 'Well, here I am. But I'm
still not sure why! What am I supposed
to say to her?' she whispered to Storm.

The puppy's luminous midnight-blue
eyes looked even brighter than usual.

'I think you should tell Janie about how
Pixie needs a home,' he woofed.

Lily frowned. 'But there's no point.
Greengates isn't a livery stable. It's a
riding school. And anyway, Janie hasn't
got room for any extra ponies. All the
loose boxes are full.'

Storm pricked his ears. 'Not all of
them.'

Lily blinked as the penny dropped.
'You're right! Bandit's not here any
more.'

Storm nodded, looking very pleased with himself.

Before Lily could ask him anything else, Janie came out into the yard. 'Lily? This is a nice surprise. What can I do for you?' she said.

'I . . . um . . .' Lily bit her lip, feeling herself going red as she struggled to find the right words to say. Now that she was here, her mind seemed to have become a complete blank.

# ★ Chapter ★
# EIGHT

Storm gave a gentle woof and as Lily looked down into his sparkling midnight-blue eyes, she felt herself starting to calm down.

Lily took a deep breath and suddenly it all came pouring out. 'I . . . um . . . wanted to ask you something. I've got a friend called Adjoa who's got a pony called Pixie. She's lovely and very sweet-natured, but the farmer who owns her field is selling up. And I thought, well, I was hoping –'

Janie smiled. 'Whoa! Slow down a bit. Let's go into my office, Lily. I could do with a break from working on my accounts. We'll have a cold drink and you can tell me all about it.'

A few minutes later, Lily sat sipping her apple juice as Janie tapped her fingers on the desk thoughtfully.

'So what you're really asking is for me to put Pixie into livery?' she said to Lily.

Lily nodded, feeling encouraged by Janie's calmness and willingness to listen. Everything seemed to have slotted into place and become clear in her mind. Now Lily knew exactly what to say.

'What about if Pixie lives here *and*
works as one of the riding school
ponies? Adjoa would have to agree, but
I think she'd do anything if it meant
she could keep Pixie. She'd still own
her, so she'd help look after her and pay
towards Pixie's food and bedding and
stuff. But it probably wouldn't cost
anywhere near as much as proper livery.'

'You seem to have got this all worked
out,' Janie said.

'I have!' Lily said firmly.

'Hmm. It could work. We've had arrangements like this in the past and we are a pony short now that Bandit's gone. But I'd have to try Pixie out before I decided that she was right for Greengates. She'd have to be gentle, friendly and dependable.'

'Oh, she is! She's perfect. Shall I ask Adjoa's parents to phone you and fix up a meeting?' Lily asked eagerly.

Janie nodded, smiling. 'Yes. You do that. You're one determined young lady, Lily Benson.'

'That's what my dad says!' Lily beamed at Janie as she got up. 'Thanks so much, Janie. Is it OK if I go and see Tinka and the other ponies? I've just got time before Mum picks me up.'

'Course it is. I'll leave you to it. I'd better get back to these accounts.'

Lily and Storm spent twenty minutes with the ponies before going back to the riding stable's entrance. Mrs Benson had just arrived and was waiting to pick her up.

On the way home in the back of the car, Lily stroked Storm's floppy sandy

ears. 'You had this all worked out, didn't you,' she said softly.

Storm nodded. 'But I could not have done it all by myself. It was you who spoke to Janie. You did it, Lily.'

Lily felt a warm glow of pride. It felt good to have helped her friend. 'I can't wait to tell Adjoa all about it. I'm going to phone her as soon as I get home.'

The moment her mum stopped on the front drive, Lily shot out of the car and made a dash for the house.

'Er, excuse me, young lady! I wouldn't mind a hand with this shopping,' her mum called after her.

'Sorry,' Lily said sheepishly.

She rushed back, grabbed some bags and dumped them on the kitchen table.

As she was coming out of the
kitchen, the hall phone rang.

It was Adjoa's mum. 'Hello, Lily. Is
Adjoa with you? Can I have a word
with her, please?' she asked.

'She isn't here,' Lily replied, puzzled.

'Oh dear, I was hoping she'd ridden
over on Pixie to see you,' Mrs Hardiker
said, sounding worried. 'Could I have a
word with your mum?'

Lily passed the phone over. 'It's Adjoa's mum.'

Lily waited impatiently while the two mums spoke. 'What's going on?' she asked as her mum replaced the phone.

'Adjoa's left a note saying she couldn't bear to give up Pixie, and some of her clothes have gone. Mrs Hardiker was hoping she'd come over here. But it's beginning to look like Adjoa's run away with Pixie.'

'Oh no!' Lily gasped.

# ★ Chapter ★
# NINE

'It'll be dark soon. Adjoa must be so scared. We have to find her and tell her the news about Greengates!' Lily said to Storm as soon as they were alone in her bedroom.

Storm nodded. 'I will take us to Adjoa's house and see if I can pick up a fresh trail.'

Lily felt a familiar warm tingling

down her back as gold sparks crackled
in Storm's sandy fur and a fountain
of golden glitter streamed out of his
tail. There was a bright flash and a
whooshing sensation and suddenly Lily
found herself standing with Storm
outside Pixie's field at the back of
Adjoa's house.

Storm sniffed around, picking up
Pixie's scent. Moments later, he
stiffened. Lily saw that his moist brown
nose was glowing like a gold nugget.
'This way!' he barked, setting off at a
run.

Lily followed Storm away from the
field and through the streets. They
hurried along the main road and then
towards the edge of town. The street
lights had already come on. Overhead

the first stars had begun twinkling in the sky.

Lily grew hot and sweaty as she and Storm followed Pixie's trail, but she wasn't tired. Gold sparks flashed past her as Storm's magic made them travel in double-quick time. Gradually Lily realized where they were heading.

'Greengates is just over there. Adjoa must have taken the bridle path. I bet she's planning to hide in the woods overnight. She'll probably take the short cut across the fields,' she told Storm.

A few minutes later, Storm barked and wagged his tail. 'Over there!'

In the twilight, Lily could just make out the figure of a pony and rider

against the shadowy hedgerows. The
moon came out from behind a cloud
and Lily could see more clearly. 'It's
them!' she cried.

Lily saw that Pixie was trotting
towards the familiar field gate. 'That
ditch! Adjoa's heading straight for it.
Those prickly branches have been
cleared away since I told Janie about it,
but a pony could still break her leg if
she stumbles into it. I bet she's too

upset to remember it's there and Pixie
won't see it in the dark!'

Storm's midnight-blue eyes flashed.
Another rainbow of sparks shot out
ahead of him and he leapt forward into
the stream of light. Lily felt herself
shooting through the air beside him.
She and Storm landed a few metres in
front of Adjoa and Pixie.

Lily walked forward, holding up her
arms. 'It's me, Lily! Adjoa, Stop!'

Adjoa reined Pixie in. The pony's ears
swivelled and her head came up, but
she halted calmly a few paces away
from the ditch.

'Lily! What are you doing here? How
did you find me?' Adjoa cried.

'Never mind that now,' Lily said. 'That
ditch I fell into the other day is right in

front of you. Pixie could have stumbled into it. Come over here. I have to tell you something.'

Adjoa urged Pixie over to one side, but she didn't dismount. She looked shaken, but determined. 'Thanks for reminding me about that ditch. But if you're going to try and persuade me to go back home, don't bother!' Adjoa said, looking down at Lily.

'Adjoa, listen! I've got some great news,' Lily said quickly before her friend could decide to ride on. 'I've been to see Janie at Greengates. She's willing to take Pixie into livery on condition that you let her be used for the riding school.'

'Really?' Adjoa looked stunned, but her hands loosened on the reins. Her

shoulders relaxed as she thought about it. 'I wouldn't mind little kids riding Pixie and she'd enjoy the extra exercise. Dad said she was getting a bit fat anyway. But even with Janie using Pixie for rides, it's still going to cost quite a lot to keep her stabled at Greengates. I still don't know if Mum and Dad will agree.'

Lily's face fell. She hadn't thought of this. It seemed as if there was a flaw in her brilliant plan.

Storm jumped up with his paws on Lily's leg and woofed for attention. Lily looked down at him. 'You could ask your mum and dad to help,' he suggested in a soft bark.

It was a few seconds before Storm's meaning sank in. 'That's it!' she burst out, her eyes widening.

'What is?' Adjoa said, puzzled.

'I've just had a brilliant idea. Come on, Adjoa. We're going back to talk to my parents!' She quickly outlined her plan.

A look of hope came over Adjoa's face. 'Do you think they'll agree?'

'They have to. It's Pixie's last chance,'

Lily said determinedly turning on her heel, confident that Adjoa would now follow her on Pixie. At her side, Storm gave an encouraging yap.

# ★ Chapter ★
# TEN

Later that evening, Lily sat at the
kitchen table eating a take-away pizza
with her mum and dad. Storm was
curled up beneath the table.

'You did well to persuade Adjoa to
come home,' her dad said. 'Her parents
were almost out of their minds with
worry. They've been on the phone
singing your praises. Well done, love.'

Lily felt herself blushing. 'Anyone would have done the same.'

'I'm not sure that's true,' her mum said, patting her hand. 'What I still can't work out is how you found her so quickly or got up to the field near Greengates in record time.'

'It must be all the exercise I've been doing. I'm super-fit, aren't I, Dad? Mmm. This pizza's delish!' Lily said, quickly changing the subject. She slipped a small piece under the table

97

for Storm to munch. 'Mu-um?
Da-ad?' she said in a wheedling
voice. 'I've . . . um . . . got something
to ask you.'

Her parents exchanged glances. 'I
hope this isn't about having your own
pony again!' Mrs Benson said.

'Course it's not,' Lily said brightly.

'Thank goodness for that!' her dad
said.

Lily paused for effect. 'It's about me
having half a pony!'

Mr Benson frowned. 'Run that by me
again.'

Lily grinned. 'What I really mean is
*sharing* a pony!' She explained about
Janie agreeing to take Pixie into livery
and being a riding school pony. 'But it's
still going to be quite expensive, so

Adjoa's parents might decide to sell
Pixie anyway. But they won't if we help
with the costs. And then I'd be sort of
sharing a pony with Adjoa. I'd be able
to groom Pixie and ride her sometimes.
What do you think?'

'I think Pixie's going to be one busy
pony!' her dad said, smiling. 'But it's an
interesting idea.'

Lily held her breath and had all her
fingers and toes crossed. At least her dad
hadn't said no outright like he usually
did.

'I know you, Lily. You'll want to be
up at Greengates every night, looking
after Pixie and grooming her,' said Mrs
Benson. 'I'm still worried that your
schoolwork could suffer.'

'I know I might like to do that, but I

won't, because I'll know that I have to
take turns with Adjoa,' Lily said
honestly. 'I'll just be so happy to be able
to ride Pixie sometimes – and pretend
she's all mine until I get a pony of my
own one day!'

Her mum and dad exchanged glances.

'Well, when you put it like that, it
sounds like a sensible arrangement,' her
mum said.

'And it's the only way Lily's ever
going to give us any peace! So the
answer's yes,' her dad added.

'Yay!' Lily flung herself at her parents
and gave them both huge hugs and
then did a little dance around the table.
'I can't wait to tell Adjoa!'

Storm ran out from under the table
and jumped up and down, barking

excitedly. Lily grinned and only just
managed to stop herself from bending
down and picking him up.

Later that night, Lily closed her
bedroom curtains, getting ready for bed.
  Outside in the street she saw a
couple of people taking their dogs for a

last walk. She jumped into bed and snuggled up under the duvet with Storm.

'Thanks so much for everything, Storm. You kept your promise about helping me to get a pony, even though things turned out differently to how I imagined! You're the most brilliant friend ever. We're going to have an amazing summer with Pixie and Adjoa!'

Storm tucked his head under her chin. 'I am glad I was able to help.'

Suddenly Lily heard howling and growling from outside in the street. She jumped back out of bed and peered through the bedroom curtains. The two dog walkers were struggling to control their dogs, which were straining at their leads and looking up at her bedroom.

In the light of the street lamps, the dogs' eyes looked pale and were glowing.

'That's weird . . .' Lily said, turning to Storm.

The tiny puppy was cowering in the bed. She could see him trembling with fright.

Frowning, Lily glanced outside again and saw the dogs suddenly calm down. After a moment, their puzzled owners walked on until they were out of sight.

Lily came back to Storm. As she went to stroke him she realized that he was trembling all over. 'What's wrong? Are you sick?' she asked worriedly.

Storm shook his head. His ears were laid back and his tail was tucked beneath him. 'I sense that Shadow is close. I think he used his magic, so that the dogs outside would attack me.'

Lily looked at her friend in dismay. 'Is that what he'll do if he finds you?

Storm nodded, his eyes as dull as blue stones. 'All the dogs around here will be looking for me now. I will use my magic to mask my scent. It may give me a little more time.'

Lily kissed the top of his sandy head,

breathing in his sweet puppy smell, and lay awake, hoping like mad that Storm would be safe. She didn't think she could bear it if she never saw him again.

# ★ Chapter ★
# ELEVEN

Lily woke with a start the next morning. To her relief, Storm was curled up asleep next to her.

He seemed more like his normal self, but his sparkling midnight-blue eyes were still wary. 'I will stay here and hide. I want to be sure that Shadow cannot sense where I am,' he barked.

Lily felt reluctant to leave him, but

she had promised to meet Adjoa at Greengates and help settle Pixie into her new home.

'I'll see you later,' she said, bending down to kiss the top of Storm's warm silky head.

Storm curled himself into a tight ball and didn't answer.

'Whoa, there, girl!' Janie Green said gently.

Lily and Adjoa stood watching as Janie backed Pixie out of the horse trailer, hitched to her Land Rover. 'That's it; good. Come on.'

Pixie slowly moved backwards, step by step. Finally she stood in the stable yard, her legs trembling slightly and her chestnut coat twitching.

'Good girl,' Adjoa crooned, going over to stroke Pixie's nose. 'She's feeling nervous. She's been used to living in a field by herself.'

'It's only natural for her to feel un-settled,' Janie said understandingly. 'She's used to you, so why don't you and Lily lead her around for a bit before you take her in to the loose box? Call me if you have any problems. OK?'

'OK. Thanks.' Adjoa looked over at Lily as Janie went to park her Land Rover. 'Janie's really nice, isn't she?'

Lily smiled and nodded. 'There are lots of strange new smells here. Why don't you walk Pixie past the paddock a few times? It might calm her if she smells fresh grass like in her field,' she suggested to Adjoa.

'That's a good idea.'

For the next twenty minutes Adjoa led Pixie round the yard, talking gently to her all the time.

Lily watched, trying not to think about Storm and whether he was still safe. But her worries about her tiny puppy friend kept pushing into her mind.

Pixie gradually seemed to relax.

Finally, Adjoa felt confident enough to lead her to Bandit's old loose box, which was to be her new home. Earlier, Lily had spread it with a deep layer of clean bedding. There was a hay net hanging up and clean water in a bucket.

Lily opened the door wide.

Adjoa went to lead Pixie inside. But Pixie rolled her eyes and stood still. 'Come on. It's lovely in there. There's space for you to turn round and lie down if you want to,' she encouraged.

Pixie shifted nervously and rolled her eyes. 'She's just not keen on going indoors,' Adjoa said.

'I'll get a bit of carrot from the feed store. That might tempt her in,' Lily said.

'Good idea,' Adjoa said gratefully.

Lily returned quickly. But the carrot didn't work either.

'What if we can't get Pixie to go in at all?' Adjoa said worriedly. 'Janie might change her mind about her. She won't want an awkward pony at the riding school.'

'That's not going to happen. Pixie's just scared. She's going to be fine,' Lily said reassuringly, but she was starting to get concerned.

If only Storm was here. He'd calm Pixie down. But Storm had to fight his own battle, hiding from his enemy – the fierce wolf Shadow.

'I think I'd better go and get Janie or Don, after all,' Lily decided reluctantly after another fifteen minutes of leading

Pixie about and a second failed attempt at getting her to go into her box.

'OK, then.' Adjoa was almost in tears.

Just then Lily heard a rustling sound from inside the loose box. A spurt of bright golden sparks shot up out of the straw and a cheeky sandy face appeared.

'Storm!' Lily exclaimed delightedly and then realized that Adjoa was giving her a strange look. 'I mean . . . it looks like rain or something. I think we should try Pixie once more before we go and get help.'

Adjoa looked doubtful, but she nodded.

Pixie stretched out her neck and blew a warm breath towards Storm. Storm barked encouragingly and wagged his tail.

Pixie lifted one front leg. She took a step forward and then another one. She went inside and Adjoa closed the door after her. 'Phew! At last! I thought she'd never go in,' she said, relieved.

'She'll be fine now. Why don't you go and tell Janie?' Lily suggested.

Just as Adjoa disappeared into the office, Storm whined in terror. He leapt over the stable door into the yard, trailing a bright comet's tail of golden sparks and streaked towards the tack room.

Lily whipped round and saw two
small dogs coming through the main
gates. They raised their heads and
she saw their abnormally long teeth
and fierce pale wolf eyes. Her heart
missed a beat. They were here for
Storm!

She dashed across the yard and rushed
into the empty tack room.

There was a bright golden flash.
Lily blinked hard as her sight cleared.
Storm stood there as his magnificent
real self. The majestic young wolf's
dazzling silver-grey fur gleamed and
his midnight-blue eyes glowed like
sapphires. A she-wolf with a gentle tired
face stood next to Storm.

And then Lily knew that this time
Storm was leaving for good.

'Our enemies are very close. We must go!' Storm's mother rumbled.

Storm raised a large silver paw in farewell. 'You have been a good friend. Be of good heart, Lily,' he said in a deep velvety growl.

Lily's throat closed with tears and there was an ache in her chest. She was going to miss Storm terribly. 'Goodbye,

Storm. Take care. I'll never forget you,' she whispered hoarsely.

There was a final bright flash and a crackle of gold sparks that sprinkled down around her like warm rain. Storm and his mother faded and then disappeared. The dogs ran into the tack room. Lily saw their teeth and eyes instantly return to normal before they turned and slunk away.

Lily blinked away tears as she went slowly back out into the yard. At least she'd had a chance to say goodbye to Storm. She knew she'd never forget the wonderful adventure she'd shared with the magic puppy.

Although she could never tell another person about Storm, there was someone else who was going to miss the tiny puppy and with whom she could share all her thoughts. Pixie!

As Lily went towards Pixie's stall and saw Adjoa coming out of Janie's office, she smiled at the thought of all the adventures they were going to have with their very own pony!

# MAGIC puppy

# Muddy
# Paws

*To Petra — a gentle sheepdog friend
and a loyal companion*

# Prologue

Storm paused to lap up thirstily the clear water that flowed swiftly between two banks of ice. It felt good to be back in his home world.

But the young silver-grey wolf's happiness lasted for only a moment as he thought of his mother, Canista, wounded and in hiding.

Suddenly a terrifying howl echoed on the icy wind.

'Shadow!' Storm gasped, realizing that the fierce lone wolf was close.

There was a bright flash and a dazzling shower of golden sparks. Where Storm had been standing there now crouched a tiny fluffy black-and-white Border collie puppy with midnight-blue eyes.

Storm trembled, hoping that his puppy disguise would protect him from the evil Shadow. Keeping his little belly low to the ground, Storm crept into a clump of snow-covered bushes.

A dark shape pushed through the bushes, loosening a cloud of snow, and Storm's tiny heart missed a beat. Shadow had found him!

But instead of the lone wolf's dark-
grey muzzle and pitiless black eyes,
Storm saw a familiar silver-grey face
with bright golden eyes.

'Mother!' he yapped with relief.

'I am glad you are safe and well, my
son, but you have returned at a
dangerous time,' Canista said in a warm
velvety growl. She nuzzled the disguised
cub's black-and-white face, but then
gave a sharp wince of pain.

'Shadow's poisonous bite sapped your
strength!' Storm blew out a gentle
stream of tiny gold sparks, which sank
into Canista's injured leg and
disappeared.

'Thank you, Storm. The pain is
easing. But there isn't time right now
for you to help me recover all my

powers. You must go – Shadow is very close,' Canista rumbled softly.

Sadness rippled through Storm's tiny puppy body as he thought of his dead father and litter brothers and the once proud Moon-claw wolf pack, now broken up. His midnight-blue eyes flashed with anger. 'One day I will stand beside you and face Shadow!'

Canista nodded proudly. 'But until then, you must hide in the other world. Use this disguise and return when your magic is stronger.'

Another fierce howl split the air. 'I know you are close! Come out and let us finish this!' Shadow cried in an icy growl.

'Go now, Storm! Save yourself!' Canista urged.

Bright gold sparks ignited in the tiny
black-and-white puppy's fur. Storm
whined softly as he felt the power
building inside him. Golden light
pooled brightly around him. And grew
brighter . . .

# ★ Chapter ★
# ONE

Beth Hollis woke with a start and lay looking up at the unfamiliar white ceiling with its low black beams. Rain pattered against the window and she could hear birdsong, animal noises and voices outside.

Gradually Beth recognized the attic bedroom in Tail End Farm owned by her aunt and uncle. She was staying here while her parents were away.

The room was still quite dark and a gust of wind sent more rain drumming against the window. Beth pulled the duvet over her head and snuggled back under the downy warmth.

Suddenly the bedroom door banged open. Beth heard muffled footsteps approaching the bed and then she felt a

rush of cool air as the duvet was
twitched aside.

'Rise and shine!' cried a cheeky voice.
'Mornings start early on a farm!'

'Hey!' Beth complained, sitting bolt
upright.

Martin Badby, her tall dark-haired
cousin, stood grinning mischievously
down at her.

'Give that back!' Beth demanded,
lungeing at him with outstretched
arms.

'No chance!' Martin crowed, backing
away. He tossed the duvet across the
room out of her reach.

Beth scowled. Martin was twelve
years old, older than her by three years,
but he sometimes acted as if he was
aged about six. He loved playing silly

jokes on people, especially his younger cousin.

'That was a really mean thing to do!' she fumed.

'Yeah? So sue me!' Martin said cheerfully. 'Are you coming downstairs, then?'

Beth sat in the middle of her bed and crossed her arms. 'No, I am not! Auntie Em said I needn't get up early on my first day here!'

'That's only cos you were sulking last night. I heard you talking to your mum and dad before they left. "Poor me. It's *so* awful having to stay at boring old Tail End,"' he mimicked in a silly whiny little voice.

'I don't talk like that!' Beth said, feeling her cheeks redden. 'Anyway, how

would you like it if you got dumped
on relatives while your parents flew off
to America for two weeks?'

Martin rolled his eyes. 'They're not
exactly going to Disney World, are
they? It's only some boring old business
trip.'

'I still wanted to go with them,' Beth
murmured. She'd never been apart from
her parents, except for the occasional
night's sleepover at a friend's house and
she was really going to miss them.

'Talk about selfish. I don't s'pose you
even thought about me?' Martin
grumbled.

Beth frowned, puzzled. 'What about
you?'

'Well, *I've* got to put up with *you*,
haven't I? Mum and Dad have

practically ordered me to look after you.
Just what I wanted, my dopey spoiled
cousin trailing round after me – not!'

'Thanks very much! I'll try not to get
in your way!' Beth cried indignantly.
She flung herself off the bed and
stomped over to the wardrobe. 'Can you
go out now, please? I want to get
dressed.'

'Thought you weren't getting up?'
Martin crowed.

'I've changed my mind. Spoiled
cousins do that a lot, you know!' Beth
said spiritedly.

'Whatever!' Martin went out and
closed the bedroom door behind him.

Beth pulled a face at the closed door.
She'd forgotten just how annoying her
cousin could be and now it seemed that

he wasn't keen on having her here at all. Her spirits sank even further as she thought of the two weeks stretching endlessly ahead of her.

'Morning, Beth. You're up early. Did you sleep well?' Emily Badby called from the yard as Beth stood in the open doorway of the back porch.

'Fine, thanks,' Beth replied. *No thanks to Martin*, she thought.

Her aunt held a bucket of vegetable trimmings. 'Goats love a nibble of fresh food. It gets them in a good mood for milking. Do you want to come and watch?'

'OK,' Beth said, shrugging. She wasn't that interested in goats, but there was still ages before breakfast and nothing much else to do.

She borrowed a spare mac and some wellies and followed her aunt into the barn. A sweetish musty smell of goats, dung and warm hay greeted her. 'Phew!' Beth wrinkled her nose.

Emily Badby laughed. 'It's a healthy farm smell. You'll get used to it.'

Beth wasn't sure she wanted to. She

went to look at the brown-and-white goats in their neat pens, ranged down one side of the barn. 'They all look a bit fed up. What sort are they?' she asked.

'Anglo-Nubians. It's their long noses and lop ears that give them that expression,' Emily explained, selecting a goat and leading it to a small wooden platform. The goat leapt up nimbly and soon Beth was watching the creamy milk foaming into a spotlessly clean bucket. 'I sell milk, yogurt and cheese in the local shops,' Emily said. 'My dairy's next door. You can have a look round sometime, but ask me first. I have strict rules about hygiene.'

Beth nodded.

Her aunt soon finished milking. She

then poured the milk through a filter into a metal churn. 'I'll just take this to the dairy and then get started on breakfast.'

A loud braying noise came from the back of the barn. 'Oh! What's that?' Beth looked round in surprise.

Her aunt laughed. 'That's Darcy, my new billy goat. He's only been here for a week or so, but he's always complaining because he isn't getting any attention.'

'Can I go and say hello to him?' Beth asked.

'Yes, of course, but be –' The rest of her aunt's reply was drowned out by a loud irritable voice in the doorway.

'There you are!' Martin cried,

standing aside as his mum went out.
'What are you hiding in here for?'

'I wasn't hiding! Auntie Em said I
could watch her milking,' Beth said.

Martin flicked back a lock of wet
dark hair. 'Anyway, Dad said I had to
ask you if you wanted to come with
me to take Ella for a walk.' Ella was the
family's old black-and-white Welsh
Border collie.

'No thanks,' Beth said, feeling miffed
that he'd only asked her because his dad
had made him. Turning on her heel, she
went towards the back of the barn. 'I'm
going to look at Darcy.'

'Hang on! I'll come with you. Ella
won't mind waiting for her walk. I
have to drag her out half the time
anyway. Since Dad retired her from

farm work, she's really stiffened up,'
Martin said.

Darcy's pen was behind some straw
bales. He was a handsome dark-brown
goat with a white neck. 'It looks as if
he's wearing a smart white collar!' Beth
exclaimed as Darcy lifted his head and
gave an inquisitive snicker.

Martin undid the latch and gestured

for Beth to go into the pen ahead of him.

Beth hesitated. 'Are you sure it's safe to go in?'

'Course,' Martin said. 'Are you chicken or what?'

Beth took two steps into the pen. Suddenly, she felt Martin shove her in the back and heard the gate slam shut. She shot forward and almost went sprawling in the straw.

'You idiot!' she cried, whirling round just in time to see Martin jogging away through the barn. 'That's not funny!' she shouted after him.

There was a bawl of protest from behind her. Beth turned back to see Darcy curling his lips and eyeing her suspiciously.

She swallowed. 'N-nice goat.'

Darcy lowered his head. He looked like he was going to charge!

# ★ Chapter ★
# TWO

Beth's heart rose into her mouth.
Suddenly there was a dazzling flash of
gold light and a big shower of bright
gold sparks sprinkled all around her and
Darcy. Blinded for a moment, she
rubbed her eyes. Beth tensed as she felt
a peculiar warm, tingly feeling down
her spine.

When she could see again, she

noticed that Darcy was frozen to the
spot and standing between the goat's
legs was a tiny fluffy black-and-white
puppy with enormous midnight-blue
eyes. Specks of gold dust seemed to be
glimmering among its fur.

'What's going on?' Beth exclaimed.

The tiny puppy drew itself up. 'I am
Storm of the Moon-claw pack. I have
arrived from a place that is far from
here.'

'Y-you can talk?' Beth gasped in total amazement.

Suddenly, the penny dropped. This was obviously another of her cousin's practical jokes. She looked around, expecting Martin to jump out triumphantly.

But there was no sign of him. Beth slowly looked back to where Storm was blinking up at her, and Darcy was still standing as if he was carved from stone.

'I don't get this,' she said, puzzled.

The fluffy black-and-white puppy took a few steps towards her on big soft paws that seemed too large for his tiny body. 'I used my magic to stop this animal before it could hurt you,' Storm woofed. 'Who are you?'

'I'm B–Beth H–Hollis,' Beth
stammered.

Storm bowed his head. 'I am
honoured to meet you, Beth.'

Beth was still having trouble taking
this in. 'Um . . . me too. But . . . who
are you? *What* are you?'

Storm didn't answer. Instead, there
was another bright golden flash.

'Oh!' Beth found herself outside
Darcy's pen. Behind her the goat
snickered contentedly and she heard
him moving about in the straw,
obviously none the worse for being
temporarily put on hold.

Beth looked around for the puppy.
But it had disappeared and standing in
its place outside the pen with her there
crouched a magnificent young silver-

grey wolf with glowing midnight–blue eyes. Large gold sparks glowed in the thick ruff round his neck.

Beth gasped, eyeing the wolf's sharp teeth. 'Storm?'

'Yes, it is me, Beth. Do not be afraid,' Storm said in a deep velvety growl.

Before Beth could get used to the sight of the amazing young wolf there was a final dazzling flash of gold light

and Storm was once again a tiny fluffy black-and-white puppy.

'Wow! That's an amazing disguise. No one would ever know you're a wolf!' Beth exclaimed. 'But who are you hiding from?'

Storm began to tremble all over and his deep-blue eyes shone with anger and fear. 'Shadow is a fierce lone wolf who killed my father and all my brothers and wounded my mother with his poisoned bite. Now Shadow is looking for me. Can you help me, Beth?'

'Of course I will!' Beth's soft heart went out to him. Storm was impressive as a young wolf, but he was adorable as a tiny helpless puppy. She bent down to pick him up. 'I'll ask Auntie Em if you can stay in my room,' she said, stroking his soft little ears.

Storm leaned up to lick her chin. 'Thank you, Beth.'

'Just wait until I tell Martin about you! He's going to be so jealous!'

'No, Beth! You must tell no one my secret!' Storm said, his tiny black-and-white face very serious.

Beth didn't want to do anything that would put her new friend in danger. Besides, she reasoned, Martin had been such a pain recently that he didn't deserve to know about Storm anyway. 'OK, then,' she decided. 'It's just you and me. I promise.'

'Aren't you a bit old to be talking to an imaginary friend?' Martin said, suddenly appearing from behind the

straw bales. His eyes widened when he
saw Storm. 'Where did that cute puppy
come from?'

'I just found him. He said his name's
–' Beth stopped quickly as she realized
that she was going to have to be a lot
more careful about keeping Storm's
secret. 'I mean I'm going to call him
Storm.'

Martin's face softened for an instant.

'Ella looked just like that when she was a puppy. He must be a Border collie too. Give him to me, then.'

'I think I'll hold on to him. He's still a bit scared,' Beth said.

Martin frowned. 'Anyone would think he's yours. This is my barn, so Storm obviously belongs to me. Hand him over!' he ordered.

Beth hesitated, annoyed at being bossed about again. Martin hadn't even bothered to ask if she was OK after he'd shoved her into Darcy's pen.

'Do not worry, Beth. Do as he says,' Storm woofed.

Beth blinked in astonishment. What was Storm doing, talking to her when Martin was so close? But her cousin didn't seem to have noticed anything strange. *I hope you know what you're doing, Storm*, she thought as she reluctantly held him out towards Martin.

Smiling triumphantly, Martin went to grab Storm, but the moment he touched his black-and-white fur he jumped backwards. 'Ye-oww!' he yelled, shaking his hands in the air. 'Something just stung me! Has he got a stinging nettle in his fur or something?'

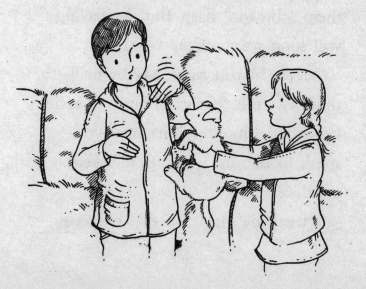

Beth pulled Storm back and held him closely again. 'I'll have a look. Maybe you should go and ask Auntie Em for some antiseptic cream.'

'Er . . . yeah,' Martin nodded as he went off, still rubbing at his hands.

'Storm!' Beth scolded gently. 'You gave him a prickle from your invisible gold sparks, didn't you?'

Storm's blue eyes twinkled mischievously. 'I think I may have made them a bit too sharp. But the feeling will soon wear off,' he woofed.

'Serves Martin right. Maybe he'll think twice before grabbing you again! But how come he didn't hear you speak to me just now?' Beth asked, puzzled.

'I used my magic, so that only you

30

can hear me.' Storm snuggled up in Beth's arms.

'You can do that? So I can hear you, but everyone else just hears you barking? Cool!' Beth kissed the top of his soft little head. 'Let's go and find Auntie Em. Breakfast should be almost ready. I bet you're hungry after your long journey.'

Storm's tummy rumbled and he gave an eager little bark.

As Beth went towards the farmhouse, she smiled. Her boring two weeks at Tail End Farm looked like they were going to be a lot more fun with Storm around!

# ★ Chapter ★
# THREE

'I wonder where he came from,' Emily
said thoughtfully after Beth finished
telling her about Storm. 'We're quite a
way from any houses out here.'

Beth looked across to where Storm
was chomping a dish of dog food. Ella,
the old collie, lay curled in her basket
watching the puppy.

'I bet Storm was abandoned. His

owners were probably hoping some
kind person would give him a home.
Like you, Auntie Em,' Beth said
hopefully.

'I really hate people who treat animals
like that,' Martin said.

'Me too!' Beth said with feeling. It
was the first time she and Martin had
agreed on anything.

They all sat at the kitchen table,
tucking into huge farmhouse breakfasts
and big mugs of tea.

'I'm not sure it's a good time to have
a stray puppy getting under everyone's
feet,' Beth's uncle said. 'We're very busy
on the farm and no one's got time to
train him. Maybe we should take Storm
straight to the pet care centre.'

Beth's heart pounded. He couldn't

mean it! She'd only just found Storm –
she couldn't bear to lose her new friend
so quickly.

Suddenly Ella gave a rusty-sounding
bark. She got up and limped stiffly over
to Storm. The tiny puppy whined softly,
wagging his tail and wriggling his fat
little body as the old dog bent down
and gave him an experimental sniff.
Ella's eyes softened and she began
licking Storm's head.

Martin's face lit up. 'Look at that! Ella's telling us that she'll keep Storm in check. She won't let him be a pest around the farm. Way to go, old girl!'

Everyone laughed.

Beth looked at her uncle and aunt. 'So, can Storm stay? He can live in my room and I'll take him home when Mum and Dad come to fetch me,' she pleaded.

'In that case, it's fine with me. If it's OK with you, Emily,' Oliver said to his wife.

Beth's aunt gave a wry smile, but she nodded.

Beth shot over and hugged her aunt and uncle. 'Yay! Thanks a million!'

She felt so pleased that she was even ready to forgive Martin for playing mean tricks on her, but there was still one thing she wanted to tackle him about first.

Beth waited until she, Martin, Storm and Ella were walking across the fields before bringing the subject up. 'I think you should apologize for pushing me into Darcy's pen. It was a rotten thing to do,' she exclaimed.

Martin's eyes widened. 'Are you still going on about that? Can't you take a joke? Girls *always* make such a fuss.'

'Yes, because boys do such stupid things!' Beth retorted. 'I thought Darcy was going to charge at me. If it hadn't been for St– Anyway, I was lucky to get out unhurt.'

But Martin wasn't listening. He had

turned round to wait for Ella who was lagging behind. The old collie was walking stiffly with her head drooping. 'Come on, girl!' he called fondly.

At the sound of his voice, Ella tried to quicken her step, but her back legs gave way and she sat down.

'She's been doing that more and more lately,' Martin said, frowning.

Beth's anger with Martin melted away as her heart stirred with sadness at the sight of the sick old dog.

Storm glanced up at her with softly glowing eyes. 'I will fetch Ella!' he woofed gently.

Beth stood beside Martin and they watched Storm bound down the field. As soon as Storm reached the old sheepdog, he whined encouragingly and

licked Ella's grey muzzle. When she just
lay there panting, Storm crouched down
on to his front paws and stuck his
bottom in the air, inviting her to play
chase.

Martin smiled at the cheeky pup's
antics. 'You're wasting your time,
Storm. Ella's dashing-about days are
*well* over!' he called, but then his face
fell and his eyes looked sad and
troubled.

Beth reached out to pat his arm.

'I'm OK. Don't fuss!' Martin said,
dashing a sleeve across his face.

Beth saw Storm running back and
forth in front of Ella, woofing gently to
encourage her until she finally heaved
herself to her feet. As the old collie
limped up the field, Storm ambled

alongside her, keeping pace on his short legs.

'Here she comes. Good girl,' Martin crooned, stroking Ella's ears.

'Thanks, Storm,' Beth whispered to him. 'Martin might be the most annoying person in the universe, but he really loves Ella.'

The four of them walked slowly back to the farmyard in silence. As they came through the gate into the yard, Martin turned to Beth. 'Do you want to see the dairy?' he said more cheerfully.

Beth shrugged. 'I don't mind. But I thought we weren't allowed in there without permission.'

'No problem. I told Mum we might go in and she was fine about it.' Martin opened the door of a brick building, next to the barn. 'But dogs are definitely not allowed. Stay, Ella,' he ordered.

Ella sat down obediently.

'Will you wait here, please, Storm?' Beth whispered, so Martin couldn't hear. 'I won't be long.'

Storm immediately plonked down next to Ella and lay with his nose on his paws.

Martin smiled. 'Storm really catches on quickly, doesn't he? Look how he copies what Ella does. He's one bright pup!'

Beth smiled to herself. If only Martin knew how right he was!

Inside the dairy it was cool and spotlessly clean. Beth walked around, looking at the white work surfaces,

shiny metal equipment and huge
fridges, being careful not to touch
anything.

But Martin was just the opposite.
'I haven't been in here for ages. I'd
forgotten that some of this stuff's pretty
high-tech. I wonder what these do.' He
began turning some dials on a big
drum-shaped machine.

There was an ominous glugging noise.

'Should you be fiddling with that?'
Beth asked worriedly.

Martin grinned. 'You're such a
scaredy-cat. Don't panic. I'm putting the
settings back to what they were.' He
turned the dial again and the glugging
noise got louder.

*Gloop. Gloop. Whoosh!* Suddenly a
fountain of milk gushed out of a

narrow chute and poured on to the
floor.

'Oh heck!' Martin cried, frantically
twiddling, but the milk only sprayed
out faster.

Beth stood there in horror as a rising
tide of milk swirled round her wellies.
'Do something, Martin!'

'I'm trying to!' Martin's face was
bright red.

The door banged open and Emily
Badby swept into the dairy. Taking in
the situation with one look, she
marched over to the machine and
adjusted the dials. Seconds later, the
flow of milk slowed and then stopped.

Emily turned round with a furious
look on her face.

'Beth told me to do it!' Martin cried,
before his mum could speak.

Beth's jaw dropped. 'No, I didn't!'

Martin smirked. 'Yes, you did! Don't
try and wheedle your way out of it –'

'Be quiet! Both of you.' Emily
snapped. 'I'm very disappointed in you
both. You're not even supposed to be in
here without permission!'

Beth glared furiously at Martin. She
was really tempted to tell her aunt how

he had fibbed about having permission
to come in here, but she'd never been a
snitch and she wasn't about to start
now.

'You know the house rules perfectly
well, Martin. Besides, Beth is our guest,'
Emily said stiffly, still furious. 'What
have you got to say for yourself?'

Martin shrugged. 'Chill out, Mum!
Don't have a major stressy! It's only a
bit of old milk. It won't take long to
clean up.'

'You think so?' Emily's face darkened.
'Stay there, you two! Don't you dare
move!' She sloshed through the milk
and opened a cupboard. 'Here!' She
thrust mops and buckets at Martin and
Beth. 'I want that floor spotless. Do you
hear me? I'd stand and watch you, but I

have to go out now. I'll be back in an
hour, though, to check up on you. And
if you touch anything else, Martin
Badby, I'll . . . I'll have your guts for
garters!'

She swept out and a few seconds later
Beth heard a car start up and drive
away.

'Flipping heck!' Beth said, letting out
a huge sigh of relief. She'd never seen

her aunt so angry. 'I thought she was going to explode!'

'Oh, Mum's never cross for long. She'll have forgotten all about it by this evening. You don't mind cleaning up by yourself, do you? I've just remembered I've got something important to talk to Dad about,' Martin said, splashing milk everywhere as he made for the door.

'Hey! Come back –' Beth cried indignantly, but Martin had already left.

Her spirits sank as she looked down at the lake of milk. It was everywhere: under the work surfaces, sloshing round the machinery and even leaking out under the door into the yard. She hardly knew where to begin.

'Thanks for nothing, Martin,' she grumbled, angry that she'd bothered to save him from being in even more trouble with her aunt.

'I will help you, Beth!' Storm woofed eagerly from the open doorway.

Beth felt a warm prickling sensation down her spine. Something very strange was about to happen.

# ★ Chapter ★
# FOUR

Big gold sparks ignited in Storm's fluffy
black-and-white fur and his ears and
tail crackled with electricity.

Storm raised a big black front paw
and a spurt of golden sparks shot out
and whooshed round the dairy. They
zizzed about like a swarm of busy
worker bees.

Beth heard a series of faint pops as a

shimmering army of mops appeared
out of thin air and stood to attention.
As if at an invisible signal, they
began mopping the floor up and
down in neat ranks. In perfect time,
they squeezed their milky heads
into each bucket in turn. *Swish!*
*Swoosh!*

'This is great!' Beth said, clapping her hands with glee as the ranks of mops did their work.

In no time at all, the dairy floor was spotless. The magic mops stood to attention once more and then disappeared in a final cascade of golden sparks.

'Wow! Thanks, Storm, that was brilliant!' Beth went over and gave him a cuddle.

'You are welcome,' Storm barked happily. 'But I saw Martin going into the house. Why did he not help you?'

'That's what I want to know,' Beth said crossly. 'He made some lame excuse about talking to his dad about something. I've just about had enough of my rotten cousin. Come on, Storm, let's go and find him. I've got a few things I want to say to him!'

Storm yapped in agreement.

As Beth charged into the house with Storm towards the sitting room, she heard Uncle Ollie's voice coming through the open door and stopped in her tracks.

'It's really not fair to let Ella go on like this. She's in pain and she can hardly get about. I think it's time we called the vet in and put her to sleep,' he was saying.

'No! Please wait, Dad. Let's leave her for just a bit longer,' Martin pleaded, sounding as if he was very close to tears.

'I'm sorry, Martin. I know you love

Ella, but I'm not prepared to let
any animal suffer, however hard it
is for you to accept. We have to think
what's best for Ella. Why don't we
talk about it again tomorrow. All
right?' Oliver Badby said gently.

'OK. But I'm not changing my mind
about calling the vet and you can't
make me!' Martin said in a choked
voice.

Beth didn't wait to hear the rest of
the conversation. She already felt a bit
guilty for listening. 'Come on, Storm,'
she whispered, tiptoeing away.

Storm trotted at her heel as she
went into the kitchen. Beth felt her
anger drain away again, just like
when they were in the field earlier.
However annoying her cousin was,

she wouldn't wish that on anyone.

'Martin was actually telling the truth this time. He really did want to talk to his dad about something important. Ella must be very sick if Uncle Ollie thinks the vet should put her to sleep. Poor old girl,' she said to Storm.

Storm nodded, his midnight-blue eyes sad.

Ella was curled up in her basket in the warm alcove. As Beth bent down to stroke her, the old dog's tail thumped against the floor.

Beth felt tears pricking her eyes. 'It's a shame that Ella's in such pain. If she wasn't, she'd be able to enjoy a few more months with Martin.'

Storm pricked his ears. 'I might be able to help!'

Beth blinked at him. 'Really? Can you use your magic to make her young again?' she asked hopefully.

'I am sorry, Beth. No magic can do that,' Storm woofed gently. He padded over and stood in front of Ella.

Once again, Beth felt the warm tingling sensation down her spine.

Big gold sparks ignited in Storm's fluffy black-and-white fur and the tips of his ears sparked with magical power. She watched as he huffed out a warm glittery breath.

A shimmering golden mist surrounded the old collie. For a few seconds, pinpricks of gold danced all around her like miniature fireflies and

then they sank into Ella's dull fur and disappeared.

Beth waited expectantly, but nothing happened. Ella looked just the same, with her grey muzzle and faded eyes.

Storm's magic didn't seem to have worked.

'Never mind. You tried. I guess magic can't be expected to do everything,' Beth said to Storm, trying hard to hide her disappointment as the last golden spark faded from Ella's fur. 'Let's go into the sitting room and find Martin. He's probably feeling really down. Maybe we can cheer him up.'

Storm had a gleam in his eye, but he just nodded. 'You have a very kind heart, Beth.'

'Anyone would do the same,' Beth

said, blushing. She always got embarrassed when people paid her compliments.

Martin was lying glumly on the sofa. Behind it, Beth could see the cabinet displaying the cups and trophies her uncle had won in ploughing competitions.

Oliver Badby sat at the table, working at the computer. He looked up and smiled as Beth and Storm came in. 'Hello. What have you two been up to?'

'We . . . I've finished cleaning up all the milk in the dairy. I thought Martin might like to go out with us or something,' Beth said.

Her uncle frowned and glanced at Martin. 'What's that about milk?'

'Er . . . nothing!' Martin said

hurriedly, getting up in a rush and hustling Beth out. 'Come on, Beth. Let's go and see if Mum needs any help with her shopping.'

'But she's not even back yet . . .' Beth protested, shaking off his arm.

'Duh! I know that! But Dad doesn't, does he?' Martin scoffed. 'And why did you have to mention the milk?'

But once in the hall, his shoulders slumped. 'Dad's been talking about taking Ella to the vet, to . . . to –'

'I know. I heard you talking to him,' Beth interrupted, feeling a lump rise in her throat. 'I'm so sorry.'

Martin shuffled his feet. 'Yeah, well. I know Ella's old and everything and I'm not ready to let her go, but Dad could be . . .' He lifted his head and looked

past Beth into the kitchen. She saw an expression of complete amazement come over his face. 'I don't believe it!'

'What?' Beth whipped round and saw Ella padding out of the kitchen. The old dog was moving easily. Her coat looked glossy and her eyes were bright and alert.

Ella trotted up to Martin and jumped up to be stroked. 'Groof!' she barked

happily, wagging her tail and giving him
a wide doggy grin.

'Look at her! It's like a miracle. She's
not even limping!' Martin threw his
arms round Ella and hugged her,
burying his face in her fur.

Ella whined, licking him all over his
face.

'Just wait until Dad sees her! There's
no way he'll be taking her to the vet
now!' Martin's face was lit up like a
Halloween pumpkin.

Beth beamed with joy as she watched
the two of them. She bent down to
stroke Storm. 'Thanks again, Storm. This
time from Martin and Ella. They're
going to have a brilliant summer
together,' she whispered.

Storm wagged his little tail happily.

# ★ Chapter ★
# FIVE

'Ella seems to have found a new lease of life since that pup arrived,' Emily Badby said as she was clearing away the lunch things the following day.

Beth was helping her aunt stack the dishwasher. She smiled, wishing that everyone knew just how true that was! But, of course, she would never tell

them or anyone else how magical
Storm was.

Oliver Badby was finishing a cup of
tea and Martin had just come back into
the kitchen after taking some food
scraps outside to the pig bin.

Storm was stretched out under the
table. Suddenly his eyes flashed with
mischief. Leaping out, he tore round
and round the huge farmhouse table,
his ears laid back and his tail streaming
behind him.

Across the room in her bed, Ella's ears
pricked up. With a spring in her step,
she shot towards the cheeky pup and
started chasing him. Storm suddenly
swerved, leapt into her empty bed and
plonked himself down. Ella jumped
straight in after him. Seconds later, the

two of them were curled up together,
licking each other.

Everyone laughed.

'That's one way to sneak into a warm
bed! You know, Ella and Storm could
almost be a mother and her puppy,'
Martin said fondly.

Then they heard the rumbling sound
of a heavy lorry drawing up outside in

the yard. Martin ran to the window and looked out.

'It's here, Dad! The Fergy's arrived!' he shouted, dashing outside.

Beth's uncle and aunt went outside to look. Beth followed curiously, wondering what was going on.

A large flatbed truck stood in the yard. On the back of it, there was a tomato-red tractor. Oliver went to speak to the lorry driver and then they began the unloading. A few minutes later, the red tractor stood in the yard.

Martin walked round it, his eyes shining. 'It's mega-ace, isn't it?'

'I s'pose it's OK,' Beth said, shrugging. She couldn't see what was so exciting about a boring old bit of farm machinery.

'OK?' Martin gave her an incredulous look. 'Are you kidding? That's a 1952 Massey Ferguson tractor.'

Beth wasn't impressed. 'It's a bit old, isn't it? Does it still work?'

Her uncle chuckled. 'Fergy's going to work very well. Wait until you see her pulling a plough. She's going to help me win the cup in the vintage class at the ploughing competition in a few weeks' time.'

'Dad's county champion at ploughing,' Martin said proudly.

To Beth, winning things for making straight lines down a field seemed like a very weird thing to do. *Don't they watch much TV around here?* she thought.

Martin saw the scornful look on her

face. He flushed. 'There's a lot of skill involved in ploughing, you know. Dad lets me have a go sometimes and I'm getting really good at it,' he boasted. 'I'm going to get a licence when I'm fourteen. Then I can compete too!'

'You're doing all right, but you'll need a lot more practice first,' his dad said.

'I know that,' Martin said in a sulky voice.

Oliver patted his son on the shoulder. 'Fergy could do with a wash and brush up. She's pretty dusty after her journey. Any volunteers?'

Martin's head came up. 'Beth and I will do it. Won't we, Beth?'

Beth frowned. Cleaning a tractor was definitely not top of her 'fun to do' list. It was right at the bottom, next to cleaning smelly trainers. But Martin seemed in an unusually good mood, so she nodded.

'OK. I don't mind.' *But if he starts bossing me about again, I'm leaving him to it*, she thought.

Beth helped Martin collect buckets, sponges and cleaning liquid. Storm came outside and lay down with his chin resting on his paws as she and Martin started work.

'There's all kinds of ploughing, you know. Tractor-trailed, mounted, reversible. You have to be very skilled to work a plot and make tidy ins and outs,' Martin explained enthusiastically as he sponged soapy water over Fergy's bright-red bonnet. 'They have world championship competitions. One day Dad might be good enough to take part.'

Beth didn't reply. She was scrubbing hard at a greasy mark on Fergy's red mudguard.

'Hey! Are you listening? Or are you ignoring me deliberately?' Martin flicked soapy water at her.

'Who said that?' Beth joked and flicked water back at him.

Martin's eyes gleamed mischievously. 'Oh yeah!'

Beth dodged out of the way as another sponge full of water sloshed towards her. 'Missed!' she crowed.

Laughing, they flicked soapy water back and forth.

Beth giggled as she pushed her damp hair out of her eyes and crouched behind the tractor. She was smaller than Martin and managed to avoid getting too wet, but most of her soapy flicks found their mark.

Martin's T-shirt was soon drenched. 'Right! Now you're for it!' He grabbed the whole bucket and lifted it into the air.

'Don't you dare!' Beth shrieked breathlessly.

As she went to flick more water at Martin, a tiny shower of golden sparks crackled around her hand and tingled against her fingers. The soapy sponge shot out of her hand. It zoomed through the air with perfect aim and splatted in Martin's face.

'Phoof!' Martin spluttered. He took a step backwards and slipped over on to his backside, tipping the entire bucket of water all over himself.

Beth cracked up laughing. She was helpless. She glanced across at Storm who wore a wide doggy grin and wagged her finger at him, scolding him gently.

'Sorry, Beth. I thought he was going to hurt you!' Storm yapped.

Scowling, Martin slowly got up. His dark hair was plastered to his head and water was dripping off the end of his nose.

At the look on his face Beth tried to stop laughing, but her mouth kept

twitching. 'You should see yourself,' she gasped, holding her ribs.

Suddenly Martin burst out laughing too. 'That was a great shot – for a girl! Come on, let's get some clean water.'

Beth went with him to fill her bucket from the outside tap. Staying at Tail End Farm was starting to feel a lot better these days.

She was amazed at Martin. This was

the most friendly he'd been since she arrived. And all because they'd had a water fight and she'd beaten him. *I'll never understand boys*, she thought, as they finished cleaning the tractor.

# ★ Chapter ★
# SIX

Beth stood in the barn beside her aunt and watched her milking the goats. Storm was sprawled on a pile of clean straw beside the pens.

Beth sighed. It had rained almost every day since she'd been here. Heavy rain was drumming on the roof once again. 'I'm getting fed up with this rotten weather,' she complained.

Emily smiled. 'You learn to take it in
your stride when you work on a farm.
But the goats really hate the cold and
the wet. That's why I brought them
into the barn, but I'd hoped they could
go out in their field again by now.' She
looked at her niece's glum face. 'Do
you want to have a go at milking?'

'I don't know,' Beth said doubtfully.

'Come on. Don't be shy. Stand here.

It's not very difficult and Daisy's a good milker,' Emily encouraged. She showed Beth how to take a firm but gentle hold and squeeze down with one finger at a time.

Beth took a deep breath and rested one shoulder against Daisy's flank. She followed instructions, a bit awkwardly at first. To her surprise, the milk began to flow into the bucket.

'Hey! I'm doing it!' she cried delightedly.

In a few minutes Beth felt like an expert. She filled a bucket and then strained the milk into the metal churn, feeling really pleased with her success. 'That was great. Maybe I'll ask Mum and Dad if we can have some goats. It would save Dad moaning about having to dig up all the weeds and we'd have loads of milk to give to all our friends.'

'Hmm. Remember that you'd have to milk them twice daily, summer and winter, seven days a week, in all weathers, just like I do,' her aunt cautioned, smiling.

Beth raised her eyebrows. 'On second thoughts, I think I'll stick to milk in cartons and leave the weeds to Dad!'

Her aunt laughed.

A loud triumphant braying came from the back of the barn. There was a stamping and clattering, followed by a rustling noise.

'Darcy?! What's he doing?' Beth said.

'It sounds like he's jumped out of his pen – again,' her aunt sighed. 'That goat's a proper menace. He's been

cooped up for too long because of all
this rain and he's got energy to spare.
I'm going to have a real game trying to
catch him.'

'Shall I help you?' Beth offered.

'You could go and see where Darcy's
got to, if you like, while I close the
barn door so he can't escape,' her aunt
said.

'I will find Darcy!' Storm barked,
darting to the back of the barn.

Beth hurried after him. As she
reached the big stack of straw bales near
the goat's pen, she spotted Darcy
standing right on the very top of them.

'Look at him! He thinks he's the king
of the castle!' Beth said.

Looking down his haughty nose,
Darcy snickered as if he agreed. He

looked very pleased with himself for
having climbed up so high.

Storm wagged his tail and then
jumped up on to his back legs and put
his front paws on the bottom bale.
'Gr-oof!' his bright eyes flashed playfully.

'Watch out, Storm. That stack looks a
bit wobbly –' Beth began warily, but
before she could finish her sentence,
Darcy flexed his powerful back legs and
did an almighty leap in the air, right
over Beth and Storm's heads – and then
everything seemed to happen all at once.

The top straw bale wobbled wildly
from the force of Darcy's take-off and
slowly began to tip forward.

Beth's eyes widened in horror. Storm
had turned his head to watch Darcy
land on the barn floor a few metres

away and hadn't noticed the danger. The
bale was about to fall and land on him!

Without a second thought, Beth
threw herself forward. Her fingers just
touched Storm's fluffy black-and-white
fur and she managed to grab him.

Holding him close to her chest Beth rolled out of the way just in time. The heavy bale crashed to the ground and she felt the rush of dusty air as it missed them both by a fraction of a centimetre.

Beth let out a shaky sigh of relief. Still holding Storm, she pushed herself slowly to her feet. 'Are you all right?' she asked the shocked little puppy.

'Yes. You saved me, Beth. Thank you,' Storm woofed, reaching up to lick her chin.

'I couldn't bear anything to happen to you,' Beth said as she stroked Storm's soft ears. She felt a surge of affection for her tiny friend.

Glancing down the barn, Beth saw that her aunt had managed to get a rope on a subdued-looking Darcy and was leading him back to his pen. She frowned when she reached Beth and Storm and saw the straw bale on the floor nearby. 'I thought I heard something fall, but I couldn't be sure with all the noise Darcy was making. Are you OK? It's lucky you weren't badly hurt,' she said.

'Oh, it missed us by miles,' Beth said

lightly, not wanting to worry her aunt.

'Thank goodness for that!' Emily said, relieved. 'I'm responsible for you while you're here and your mum and dad wouldn't be very pleased with me if you had an accident. I'll get Oliver to come and see to that stack. Just let me tether this naughty goat in his pen first. He's full of surprises.'

Beth bit back a grin. *He's not the only one!* she thought.

'I'm sorry, Martin, I haven't got time to go out with you today. Maybe tomorrow. I'm planning to clear the unused bit of the top field and use that for practising ploughing, but I can't promise when I'll get round to it,' Oliver was saying.

'Aw, Da-ad. You've already been out on Fergy a couple of times. When am I going to get the chance to have a drive?'

Beth sat in the window seat in the sitting room with Storm curled on a cushion beside her. Her uncle and cousin were in the yard outside. Their voices floated in through the open window. 'Martin's obsessed with that dumb old red tractor, even though Uncle Ollie's told him it's too big for him to drive by himself.'

Storm's ears twitched and he gave a sleepy nod, tired out from all the excitement in the barn earlier.

Two minutes later, Martin burst into the room and plonked himself down next to Beth.

'Watch it! You almost sat on Storm!' Beth complained.

'Sorry, Storm.' Martin stroked Storm's fluffy black-and-white fur absently. 'Dad's being a right pain! He won't let me near Fergy unless he's with me. I know I can handle driving her by myself, but he won't believe me,' he grumbled.

Beth wisely chose to stay silent on the matter. 'It's stopped raining at last. Why don't we walk into the village with Storm and Ella?' she suggested, trying to cheer him up.

Martin's lip curled. 'Go shopping? I'd rather watch paint dry. I'm going to take Ella for a long walk over the fields. By myself,' he said pointedly.

Beth got the message. She didn't bother to tell him that she'd been about to suggest that they went to the new sports centre. 'Suit yourself.' She shrugged, got up and called to Storm to follow her.

'Where are you going?' Martin asked, frowning.

Beth turned to him and tapped the side of her nose with one finger in what she knew was an annoying way.

Martin threw up his hands, got up and stormed out, muttering about 'stupid annoying girls' under his breath.

'Oh well. Martin's back to his usual self. His good mood didn't last long, did it?' Beth said to Storm. 'But I'm getting used to him now and I don't mind it so much. I think he just likes moaning!'

Storm nodded, blinking up at her with bright midnight-blue eyes.

Beth changed her mind about the sports centre. 'We'll go to the village by ourselves. I bet they have a pet shop that sells dog treats,' she decided.

Storm yapped excitedly, almost falling over his own paws as he bounded out of the door.

# ★ Chapter ★
## SEVEN

Emily Badby had been baking bread all morning and the whole farmhouse smelled wonderful.

Beth sat in the cosy kitchen, reading a new computer magazine she'd bought at the village shop. Storm was curled up beneath the table, chomping on a bone-shaped dog chew and Beth could feel the tiny puppy's warmth against her feet.

It had just been raining again, but a watery sun was now beginning to push through the clouds.

Suddenly the faint sound of barking and growling interrupted Beth's peaceful morning. She tensed, listening hard. It seemed to be coming from far away, but then the noise stopped and Beth thought she must have been mistaken. Her aunt didn't seem to have noticed anything.

'Where's Martin?' Beth asked.

'Up at the top field. His dad's making a start on clearing it with Fergy and the old plough. Ella's with him,' Emily replied.

Making sure her aunt wasn't looking, Beth leaned over to whisper to Storm. 'I'll take you for a walk up there later.

It's no good waiting for Martin and
Ella to come back here. Wild horses
wouldn't drag him away if Uncle Ollie's
ploughing.'

There was no reply.

Frowning, Beth bent right over and
looked under the table. Storm had gone,
leaving the half-eaten dog chew lying
there.

That was odd. He'd never run off

without telling her where he was going before. She got up and went to look for him.

Storm wasn't in the sitting room or any of the other downstairs rooms. She went up to her bedroom, expecting to find him curled up on her duvet, but he wasn't there either.

'Storm?' she said, beginning to feel concerned.

A faint sound came from beneath her pillows. Beth smiled and swept back the top of the duvet to reveal a little black-and-white tail. 'What's this, hide-and-seek –' she began, but stopped at the sight of Storm trembling all over. 'What's wrong? Are you sick?' she asked worriedly.

Storm squirmed more deeply into the

pillows. 'I sense that Shadow knows where I am. He will send his magic, so that any dogs that are nearby will attack me,' he said in a muffled little whine.

'Oh no! That must have been what I heard. We need to find you a better hiding place. Maybe the barn or . . . or . . .' Beth racked her brains trying to think of somewhere safe.

'It is no use, Beth,' Storm whimpered, his deep-blue eyes as dull as stones. 'Leave me here for a while, please. Any dogs looking for me may pass by.'

'All right. If that's best,' Beth said. She had a sudden thought. 'What about Ella? Will Shadow's magic work on her too?' She felt horrified that the gentle old collie might become Storm's enemy.

'No. I have already used my magic to

help her. That will protect Ella from Shadow's evil,' Storm whined before he burrowed right under the pillows and curled up into a tight little ball.

Beth gently gathered his tail in, replaced the duvet and tucked it tightly round him. No one would know there was anything under the pillow. She went out quietly, hoping like mad that Storm's plan would work. She couldn't

bear to think of her friend having to leave suddenly with no warning.

Beth could hardly eat any lunch for worrying about Storm. She nibbled a few mouthfuls of the delicious tomato salad and cauliflower cheese and then asked if she could leave the table.

'Are you feeling all right?' her aunt asked.

'Fine, thanks. I'm just not very hungry,' Beth replied.

Martin glanced at Beth in concern and seemed about to say something, but then he changed his mind. He finished eating and jumped up from the table.

'Why don't you and Storm come up to the top field before lunch and see how Dad and I are getting on? We've cleared quite a lot of it already. I'm going up there again now with Ella. You could come with us, if you like.'

'I might do. I'll . . . um . . . follow you up there in a minute,' Beth murmured absently.

'Please yourself,' Martin muttered.

When he and Ella had left, Beth went into the hall with a heavy heart. She was dreading going upstairs to her bedroom. Would Storm still be here or had her friend already gone forever?

Suddenly, a tiny fluffy black-and-white figure came bounding down the stairs. 'Hello, Beth,' Storm barked happily.

'Storm! You're still here!' Beth cried, overjoyed, throwing her arms round him.

Storm yapped and licked her face, his tail whirling madly. His midnight-blue eyes were as bright as a moonlit sky and he seemed completely back to his usual self. 'I cannot sense any strange dogs nearby, so they must have gone past. But if they return I may have to leave at once. We might not have time to say goodbye.'

'I understand,' Beth said, hardly taking this in. She just wanted to enjoy every single moment of the time they could now spend together.

She secretly hoped that Storm would stay with her forever, even though she knew he must someday return to help his injured mother and lead the Moon-claw wolf pack.

Beth decided to talk about something

else. 'Do you fancy going to watch Uncle Ollie giving Martin some ploughing practice? It'll probably be dead boring,' she said, pulling a face.

Storm's cute face lit up, as it always did at any chance of a walk.

*Where's Uncle Ollie?* Beth wondered as they walked towards the top field. She could see the red tractor and the plough mounted behind it, but only Martin and Ella stood beside it.

Storm was trotting beside her with his nose snuffling round on the ground.

Martin waved. 'Hi! I didn't think you'd bother coming,' he shouted, sounding surprised and pleased.

Ella spotted Storm. She wagged her tail and trotted over, barking a greeting.

'I thought we might as well. Storm loves playing with Ella,' Beth said, smiling at the dogs.

'Great. Now you can see what ploughing's all about. Watch this,' Martin called out. Leaping into Fergy's seat he started the engine and moved forward.

'Martin, don't! You're not supposed to be doing that!' Beth said worriedly, remembering her uncle's strict rules about Martin only driving under his supervision.

'I know what I'm doing!' Martin said

huffily. 'Anyway, I'll only plough a couple of furrows. Dad's just popped down to the barn for a can of lubricating oil – he'll never know. Unless you decide to tell him,' he said, looking hard at her.

'Thanks a lot. You should know by now that I don't snitch!' Beth said indignantly.

Martin looked uncomfortable and then he gave a wry grin and nodded. Concentrating hard, he held the large steering wheel steady, as the red tractor trundled slowly along, pulling the plough behind it. As he moved forward, the weedy turf was turned over and the soil curved away from the plough's metal mouldboards in rich brown waves.

Despite herself, Beth was fascinated by watching the furrows form. Martin leaned over to watch the back wheels, making sure he kept driving in a perfectly straight line. The new brown furrow folded itself over and was laid neatly next to one previously made.

Beth realized that ploughing took a lot of skill. 'You're pretty good at this, aren't you?' she said, impressed.

Martin threw her a smile over his shoulder, obviously enjoying himself and pleased by her praise. 'I'm not bad. But then I was taught by an expert. My dad!'

Suddenly Storm's head came up and his midnight-blue eyes flashed. Barking shrilly, he raced forward and began dodging back and forth in front of

Fergy's front wheels. 'Stop! Stop!' he
barked urgently.

'Martin! Watch out for Storm!' Beth
cried.

'Why's he doing that? Call him off!'
Martin shouted.

Beth frowned. It wasn't like Storm to
do something so dangerous without a
good reason. But she was too worried
about him getting hurt to try and work
out what that was.

'Come here, Storm! You'll get hurt!'
she shouted.

But Storm seemed beside himself.
Barking frantically, he ran even closer
to the tractor's ridged tyres, snapping at
them and growling. One of the wheels
passed by him closely, missing him by a
fraction.

As a stone flew out and hit him,
Storm gave a loud yelp.

'Martin! Look out!' Beth screamed,
sure that Storm was about to be run
over.

Panicking, Martin swung the tractor's
steering wheel to avoid the tiny puppy.
Fergy slewed to a halt. Martin turned
off the engine and jumped down.

'Look at that furrow. It's all wonky now. That stupid puppy's made me mess up!' he fumed.

Storm stood by, panting heavily, his little sides heaving.

'Hang on! What's that? Look!' Beth interrupted, pointing at something half buried in a weedy grass ditch that Martin had been just about to plough up. It was a brownish metal tube with a blunt end. As Beth leaned over for a closer look, her heart missed a beat. 'I think it might be a bomb!'

# ★ Chapter ★ EIGHT

'Don't be daft!' Martin said to Beth, striding over to have a look, but the moment he saw the metal object he frowned. 'Oh! You're right. It does look like a bomb. But it's probably been there for donkey's years. Look, it's all rusty and dented. I bet it's harmless.'

'Storm didn't seem to think so,' Beth reminded him.

Martin hesitated, chewing at his lip.

Beth guessed that he was worried about getting into trouble for driving the tractor. 'Martin, this is an emergency. We have to go and tell Uncle Ollie – now!' she said.

'You're right,' Martin decided. 'Come on!'

Beth didn't need telling twice. She bent down to pick up Storm and then

turned on her heel and ran. Martin and
Ella leapt after her and they all hurried
back towards the farm as fast as they
could.

Luckily Oliver was just coming
out of the barn with an oil can. He
raised his eyebrows when they raced
straight up to him. 'Where's the fire?'
he joked, but his face grew serious as
Martin and Beth began explaining.

'Well done, you two. You did the
right thing. Unexploded bombs
need expert handling. Right. I'll
phone the emergency services and
then alert the neighbours.' He took
his mobile phone out of his jacket
pocket and dialled. 'Martin, will you go
into the house and tell your mum,
please?'

Martin nodded, his face now pale
with worry.

Beth realized that her cousin had only
just begun to grasp how serious this
really was. Now that they were all a
safe distance from the bomb, she found
herself shaking as it all sank in.

'Thank goodness you sensed the
bomb was there. You were very brave
to get so close to the tractor and risk
getting hurt,' she whispered to Storm.

'I had to stop Martin somehow. We
were too close for me to use my magic.
Martin would have seen, but I could
not risk anyone getting hurt,' Storm
woofed gently.

Beth and Storm stood in the yard
with Martin, Ella and her aunt as noisy
police cars and fire engines arrived.

Farm workers and their families began gathering too.

Beth looked towards the top field, where blue lights from half a dozen police cars were now flashing. She could see at least four fire engines. Bright-yellow hazard tape had been strung all round the site of the bomb and across the field entrance.

'If it hadn't been for Storm making a pest of himself, I'd have ploughed straight over that bomb,' Martin said. He bent down to pat Storm's head. 'Thanks, boy. You might just have saved my life.'

'You are welcome, Martin,' Storm barked, wagging his tail, but of course only Beth could hear him speaking.

She beamed down at Storm, feeling

very proud of her brave little friend.

Oliver came up and put a hand on his son's shoulder. 'I should ground you for a week for driving Fergy when I particularly told you not to!' he said sternly.

'It wasn't my fault. Beth . . .' Martin started to make another excuse to get himself out of trouble, but then he seemed to think better of it and hung his head. 'Beth told me I shouldn't be driving Fergy by myself and she was right. I'm sorry, Dad.'

'You always are,' Oliver sighed. 'But on this occasion it was lucky for all of us that things have turned out this way. If I'd have been ploughing and not you, I probably wouldn't have seen the bomb until it was too late.'

Martin looked subdued as he took
this in and realized what it could have
meant. He was silent for a moment,
and then he brightened. 'So I'm not
in all that much trouble after all.
Cool!'

'I give up!' His dad shook his head
slowly and rolled his eyes.

'Look, someone in the field's waving a red flag,' Beth noticed.

Just then Oliver's mobile phone rang. He answered it and then spoke in a loud voice. 'Listen up, everyone. There's going to be a controlled explosion in a few minutes. We needn't be alarmed. We're quite safe here.'

*Whump!* A loud bang split the air.

Despite the early warning, Beth almost jumped out of her skin as the explosion echoed in her ears. An enormous spray of dark soil shot out in all directions and a thick dark plume of smoke drifted upwards.

'Yay! Way to go!' Martin shouted.

Everyone clapped and cheered. The danger was over.

'There'll be no more ploughing in

that field until the bomb squad have declared it safe. Do you hear me, Martin?' Oliver said.

'I wouldn't go up there now if you paid me,' Martin said.

Beth could see that he meant it this time. Martin really seemed to be changing and Beth realized that she'd actually grown quite fond of her grumpy cousin during her time at Tail End Farm!

'If you'd all like to come into the house I'll make coffee and there's freshly made cake,' Emily called out to everyone.

People began filing into the farmhouse. Martin called Ella to heel and followed them in. Beth was about to go in too, when Storm suddenly

whined with terror and streaked
towards the barn.

Beth heard a fierce growl behind her
and looked round. She spotted two
mongrel dogs running into the
farmyard. As Beth saw their extra-long
teeth and pale wolf-like eyes, she felt a
clutch of fear.

The dogs were under Shadow's spell.
Storm's enemy had found him!

Without a second thought, Beth raced
into the barn ahead of the dogs.
Somehow she knew where Storm
would be. Darcy's pen!

She reached the pen at the back of
the barn in time to see the tiny black-
and-white puppy running into it. As the
dogs pursuing Storm ran into the barn,
there was a snort of rage and Darcy
leapt right over the top bar of the pen
and landed on the barn floor.

Braying threateningly, the billy goat
ran straight at the fierce dogs with his
head lowered. *Bang! Thud!* He butted
them in the side, buying Storm precious
time.

Suddenly there was a blinding gold
flash and bright golden sparks rained
down all around Beth and crackled on

to the barn floor. Storm was no longer a tiny black-and-white puppy but instead stood before her as a young silver-grey wolf with glowing midnight-blue eyes. At his side was a huge she-wolf with a gentle face.

Beth knew this was the moment that Storm had to leave.

Storm lifted his magnificent head and looked at her with sad eyes. 'Be of good heart, Beth. You have been a true friend,' he growled in a deep velvety voice. He raised a large silver paw in farewell and then he and his mother faded and were gone.

There was a terrifying howl of rage behind Beth. The mongrels' teeth and eyes instantly returned to normal and the confused dogs ran out of the barn.

Beth stood alone in the barn. A deep sadness welled up in her. She couldn't believe that Storm had left so suddenly. She was glad he was safe, but she was going to miss him terribly.

'I'll never forget you, Storm,' she whispered, her throat closing with tears.

She knew that she'd always treasure the time she had shared with the tiny magic puppy.

She heard steps behind her and turned to see Darcy coming towards her. He leaned forward to nuzzle her arm. 'You were really brave. Storm would be so proud of you,' she said, stroking him before leading him back to his pen. 'The sun's coming out. I think I'll ask Aunt Em if you can go out in the field.'

Darcy snickered delightedly as if he understood.

'Talking to yourself again?' Martin joked from behind her. 'Are you coming into the farmhouse? I've saved you a piece of cake.'

As Beth turned to look at her cousin,

she grinned. *Trust Martin to have the last word*, she thought, knowing somehow that Storm was watching them, his midnight-blue eyes glowing with approval.

# MAGIC puppy

## Win a Magic Puppy goody bag!

The evil wolf Shadow has ripped out part of Storm's letter from his mother and hidden the words so that the magic puppy Storm can't find them.

### Storm needs your help!

★ Four words have been hidden in secret bones in the first four Magic Puppy books.

★ Find the hidden words and put them together to complete the message from Storm's mother.

★ Send it in to us and each month we will put every correct message in a draw and pick out one lucky winner who will receive a Magic Puppy gift – definitely worth barking about!

**Send your secret message,
name and address on a postcard to:**

Magic Puppy Competition
Puffin Books, 80 Strand, London WC2R 0RL

### Good luck!

Visit: www.puffin.co.uk/magicseriescomp
**Closing date:** 1 December 2014

# It all started with a Scarecrow.

**Puffin is seventy years old.**
Sounds ancient, doesn't it? But Puffin has never been
so lively. We're always on the lookout for the next big
idea, which is how it began all those years ago.

Penguin Books was a big idea from the mind of
a man called Allen Lane, who in 1935 invented
the quality paperback and changed the world.
**And from great Penguins, great Puffins grew,
changing the face of children's books forever.**

The first four Puffin Picture Books were hatched in 1940 and the
first Puffin story book featured a man with broomstick arms called
Worzel Gummidge. In 1967 Kaye Webb, Puffin Editor, started the
Puffin Club, promising to **'make children into readers'.**
She kept that promise and over 200,000 children became
devoted Puffineers through their quarterly instalments of
*Puffin Post*, which is now back for a new generation.

Many years from now, we hope you'll look back and
remember Puffin with a smile. **No matter what your age
or what you're into, there's a Puffin for everyone.**
The possibilities are endless, but one thing is for sure:
whether it's a picture book or a paperback, a sticker book
or a hardback, **if it's got that little Puffin
on it – it's bound to be good.**